my so simple life

Rachel Riley goes back to basics

D0195218

Other books by Joanna Nadin

My So-Called Life
The Life of Riley
The Meaning of Life

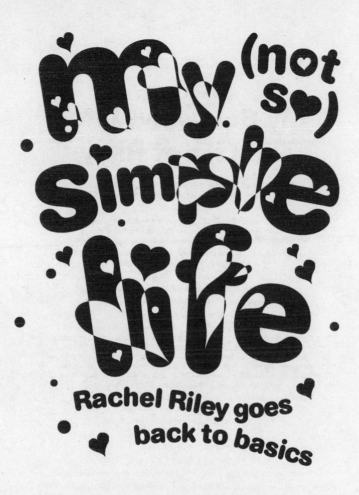

my (not so) simple life

Rachel Riley goes back to basics

Joanna Nadin

OXFORD
UNIVERSITY PRESS

OXFORD

UNIVERSITY PRESS

Great Clarendon Street, Oxford OX2 6DP

Oxford University Press is a department of the University of Oxford.
It furthers the University's objective of excellence in research, scholarship,
and education by publishing worldwide in

Oxford   New York

Auckland   Cape Town   Dar es Salaam   Hong Kong   Karachi
Kuala Lumpur   Madrid   Melbourne   Mexico City   Nairobi
New Delhi   Shanghai   Taipei   Toronto

With offices in

Argentina   Austria   Brazil   Chile   Czech Republic   France   Greece
Guatemala   Hungary   Italy   Japan   Poland   Portugal   Singapore
South Korea   Switzerland   Thailand   Turkey   Ukraine   Vietnam

Oxford is a registered trade mark of Oxford University Press
in the UK and in certain other countries

© Joanna Nadin 2009

The moral rights of the author have been asserted

Database right Oxford University Press (maker)

First published 2009

All rights reserved. No part of this publication may be reproduced,
stored in a retrieval system, or transmitted, in any form or by any means,
without the prior permission in writing of Oxford University Press,
or as expressly permitted by law, or under terms agreed with the appropriate
reprographics rights organization. Enquiries concerning reproduction
outside the scope of the above should be sent to the Rights Department,
Oxford University Press, at the address above

You must not circulate this book in any other binding or cover
and you must impose this same condition on any acquirer

British Library Cataloguing in Publication Data

Data available

ISBN: 978-0-19-272834-0

1 3 5 7 9 10 8 6 4 2

Printed in Great Britain by CPI Cox and Wyman, Reading, Berkshire

Paper used in the production of this book is a natural, recyclable product made
from wood grown in sustainable forests. The manufacturing process conforms
to the environmental regulations of the country of origin

For James
For always managing to make me laugh.
With thanks to **Karen Saunders**.
For tea, sympathy and the midget circus.

Saturday 14

8 a.m.

Today is utterly the worst day of my life, and I should be jubilant because I have been waiting for tragedy to strike my boring existence for several years but, instead, am racked by torture and loss. It is because Justin Statham, Year Twelve rock god and part-time meat mincer, stood me up on prom night for Sophie Jacobs (dad invented Microwave Muffins, was once in a Fairy Liquid advert, 34C breasts). She finally overcame her obsession with possible pervert-in-school Mr Vaughan and his oversized nipples and has returned to the hairless, small-nippled chest of her first love. It is like in *The OC* when Ryan leaves beautiful and brainy Marissa to go back out with low-rent Theresa from Chino. (Although, unlike Marissa, I am not a drug addict or lesbian. And Justin does not wear wife-beaters or play pool).

Plus Mum would not let me stay in my room all evening in case I tried to self-harm with my ironic fairy wings, so I had to watch *Poirot* with her, Dad, a ten year old in a Ninja Turtle outfit and the dog (also in Ninja Turtle outfit). James did offer to be my date but the shell was off-putting. Not to mention the potential incest issues. Am too distraught to even eat Shreddies. Will possibly pine myself to death. Even Mum feels sorry for me. She has phoned in sick to my Saturday job, i.e. hunchback Mr Goldstein and his lentil-smelling health food outlet Nuts In May, with an alleged dose of unseasonal

3

winter vomiting bug. Although she is probably secretly celebrating, as Justin was not high on her list of potential suitors due to his *a*) long hair; *b*) decision to pursue career as rock guitarist; and *c*) mum who wears Lycra. Oh God, he is even gorgeous on paper. I miss him even more. Will sob on bed for a bit.

9.15 a.m.
Have just had excellent thought. Maybe Justin did not stand me up, but is, in fact, dead. Hurrah. Will text best friend Scarlet in hope he was killed in tragic road accident on notorious mini roundabout system.

9.20 a.m.
He is not dead but is very much alive and back with Sophie Microwave Muffins. Apparently they were all over each other behind the C Corridor fruit and nut dispensing machine last night. Scarlet says she is coming round immediately for a full report and to offer sister-hood support in my time of crisis. Plus her mum Suzy is having one of her tantric sex classes in the den and she says she cannot bear all the old people groaning. It is like an X-rated version of *Cocoon*. Am still too distressed to eat. Am an accidental anorexic.

1.00 p.m.
Scarlet has just left. I asked if she wanted to stay all day. And preferably night, lest I perish in my solitude. But

4

apparently the tantric sex finished at twelve so it is safe to enter the den without fear of naked geriatrics. Plus she has E4 at home whereas our Freeview is limited to BBC4, ITV3, and BBC Parliament. It is not the signal. It is Mum's ferocious parental controls. Anyway, am too depressed to watch television due to Scarlet's over-graphic description of Justin and Sophie's love-in last night (Goth Corner Mark II, Mrs Leech's biscuit cupboard, and the upper school toilets). She knows too many technical terms for genitals.

Scarlet says I should look on the plus side, i.e. that I did not actually do 'It' with Justin, now that he is not my ONE after all. But I pointed out that, maybe if I had done 'It', then he would still be my ONE and that now am going to die a virgin like Miss Crawley with the moustache and too many cats. But then Scarlet went into one of her lectures on wearing your virginity with pride. It is because she is still not back with weedy bat boy Trevor Pledger. Apparently he snogged Daisy Devlin who has a fake Marilyn Manson tattoo behind the wheelie bins. (The snogging I mean. The tattoo is on her buttock.) Prom night was clearly a hotbed of adolescent groping. Thin Kylie and Fat Kylie and their respective boyfriends Mark Lambert and Mr Whippy did some swinging behind the fire curtain. Thank God they will all be leaving school in a few days. John Major High will be almost Eton-like without their idiotic antics tainting the corridors of intellect. Though there are still several

5

O'Gradys too many on the register. And one Justin Statham. Oh God, please let him fail his resits so he has to go and make sausages full time. I cannot bear to look upon his poetic beauty every day, when it will never again be mine to touch. Or snog. Am going to sob a bit more.

1.15 p.m.
James and dog have been in to announce that there is soup on the table. I said I was too weak to make it downstairs. He is going to bring me some in a non-spill flask.

1.20 p.m.
Oh God. Soup is oxtail. Which reminds me of butchering Justin. Am going to have to sob again.

1.25 p.m.
Sobbing has spilt soup out of non-spill flask on M&S duvet. May well have to write to Thermos to complain. Have texted Dad to send dog up to keep me company in my hour of need. Dog will lick up soup and I will be shout-free from Mum. In my weakened state, one telling off could send me over the edge.

1.30 p.m.
Dog does not like oxtail. Has eaten flask cup instead. Have sent it back down before it tries to hawk it up on already vile polycotton bedlinen.

5 p.m.
Oh God. Must have fallen asleep in post-oxtail grief. Bizarrely, duvet is now soup-free and smelling of Lenor. Maybe God has taken pity on me and performed a modern miracle. Am like that girl in Portugal who found God in an aubergine. Or Granny Clegg when she saw Jesus's face in a slice of Nimble toast (the real one, not my one-year-old uncle).

5.15 p.m.
Am not like Portuguese girl or Granny Clegg. It was James. He washed sheets while Mum was at Marjory's next door admiring her new binoculars (she has been investing heavily in surveillance equipment ever since she caught photographic evidence of me and Justin snogging on her digital camera). He is being extra specially helpful. He says it is his new Ninja way, to protect the weak and stupid. He has brought me stain-free Marmite sandwiches for supper.

6 p.m.
Have just had a phone call from Jack, (brother of Scarlet, newly appointed Head Boy, and former best friend of two-timing Justin). But have no idea what he said because before he opened his mouth, just shouted, 'Do not say, "I told you so". I hate you, Jack Stone.' Which is almost true. I hate him for being right about Justin anyway. Why did I not listen to him? It is because I was

blinded by love. And by good hair. Oh God. Need to sob. And then eat a sandwich as am quite faint now.

7 p.m.
Have eaten several sandwiches and feel slightly less suicidal. May just manage to drag self downstairs to watch some escapist TV and take mind off real-life tragedy (TVs in bedrooms are on par with heroin and murder in Mum's eyes).

9 p.m.
Am back in bed. Entire BBC schedule reminds me of Justin e.g. car crash victim in *Casualty* had Doors poster on bedroom wall, i.e. like Justin. Man from Birmingham on crap lottery show said his favourite one out of Girls Aloud was Nicola i.e. like Justin. Am going to go to sleep instead. Will probably feel better in morning.

Sunday 15
8 a.m.
Do not feel better. Am still in pit of despair. But think smell a bit so will have shower as do not want to end up malodorous as well as single, like Year Twelve bisexual Oona Rickets.

11 a.m.
Or Sad Ed. He has just been round to offer condolences

and reviving mini Mars bars. He is utterly depressed too. Though is also unwashed and quite ripe. It is because his girlfriend Tuesday has been repatriated to America. He says I should be happy I am not him. That is true. He has fat upper arms and his mum is in the Aled Jones Fan Club. No wonder he exists in a perpetual state of gloom. He says I should not be afraid of facing Justin at school, as he and Scarlet will be my henchmen. They do not stand a chance against Sophie Jacobs though. She has Pippa Newbold and Fi Cunningham, who can send Year Sevens into paroxysms with one flick of their highlighted Pantene hair.

1 p.m.
Thin Kylie has just been round to offer condolences and to set me up with Mark Lambert's friend 'Donkey' Dawson who works in Halfords and is renowned for having a weird helmet head and big thing. Have said no. Kylie says I am making a mistake and that I need to get back in the saddle immediately to make Justin jealous. I said I had never been in saddle and do not think that former Criminal and Retard with oversized head and penis will make rock god Justin weep with remorse. She said, 'Whatever. But Donkey is, like, a legend in Bishop's Stortford. It is like a saveloy.' Luckily at that point Mum came in and despatched Kylie before I had to listen to any more sausage/penis comparisons. Am going for lunch now. Still feeling weak with depression but Mum

is paranoid about me becoming anorexic so she wants to monitor every mouthful.

3 p.m.
Have not eaten lunch. It was bangers and mash. Mum is now convinced I have eating disorder. I do not. It is just that the sausages (Duchy Originals Pork and Herb) reminded me of 'Donkey' Dawson. Although I suspect his is of inferior quality and does not come with Prince Charles's seal of approval. On plus side, did not think about Justin for several minutes. Maybe I am in recovery.

3.15 p.m.
Am thinking about Justin again. Maybe I should call him. Maybe it has all been a terrible misunderstanding and there is a rational explanation for him groping Sophie's 34Cs behind the yoghurt-covered raisin display. Will ask James. He is full of Ninja insight and is well versed in conspiracy theories, thanks to his trusty companion Google.

3.30 p.m.
It is not good news, odds-wise. James says, statistically, seventy-five per cent of sexually active eighteen year olds have cheated at least once by the time they leave school. Plus my hair is mental and I have no breasts.

Also, spookily, just got a text from Jack. It says DON'T CALL HIM OR LURK OUTSIDE HOUSE LIKE STALKER X

Which is exactly what I was thinking of doing next. Although not so much like stalker, more lovelorn tragic heroine type. Maybe he has supernatural powers. That would come in useful when he is being Foreign Secretary, which is his ultimate goal, alongside winning the Mercury Music Prize for his band the Jack Stone Five. He could predict what despots and dictators are thinking and outwit them. Have texted back. Y NOT?

4.15 p.m.
Jack has replied. It says U 2 GD 4 VACANT PRETTY BOY (he means Justin).

Have texted back. NOT VACANT. BUT IS PRETTY. It is hard to believe they were ever best friends. They are so different. Justin would never accuse Jack of being vacant. Or pretty. But then Jack would never dump me on prom night for someone who was once in a Fairy Liquid advert.

4.30 p.m.
Jack has texted back. JUST DON'T DO IT RILEY. WILL EAT FONE IF HAVE TO X Which is quite funny. Although James claims Mad Harry has eaten a phone. He is hoping to become a phenomenon like fat Frenchman Monsieur Mangetout. He should take some tips from the dog. It can seemingly consume any household appliance without suffering ill effects. I caught it chewing Mum's Wisdom Spinbrush in the bathroom this morning. (Gave it a quick rinse. Mum will never know.)

11

4.45 p.m.
Jack has just texted again. It says. SERIOUSLY. DON'T.
He is very commanding when he wants to be. Have said
OK. He is right. As always. I will only be prolonging my
agony. Do not want to speak to or see Justin again.

5.00 p.m.
And could not call even if wanted to now. James has
been in to confiscate phone. He said his Ninja powers
detected that I was about to make contact with the
enemy. He means he heard beeping and got suspicious.
He is like Mum when it comes to suspecting the worst.
Am going for tea. Which will hopefully not be penis-
shaped in any way.

6 p.m.
Was quiche. So genital-free. Ate with gusto to prove Mum
wrong about anorexia. But she thinks quiche bingeing
could be sign of bulimia and has taken to hovering at
toilet door when I go for a wee. Also, James is still refusing to give back phone. He says I should be preparing
myself mentally for school tomorrow as it could be
traumatic. Oh God, he is right. I cannot go. Justin and
Sophie will be all over each other on the saggy sofa and
I will be nothing more than an object of pity and deri-
sion. It is utterly tragic. Hopefully will die in night from
sadness. If not, will have to think of cunning plan to
evade Mum's anti-truancy divining skills. She does not

allow days off unless she has forensic evidence of vomit or runny poo.

. . . .

Monday 16

Am not dead. But have cunning plan. Am going to pretend to walk to school but will actually detour to Grandpa Riley's house. He is bound to be in now that Baby Jesus is banned from Treena's place of work (The Twilight Years Day Centre) in case he is stolen by old ladies again. Plus Grandpa is notoriously lax about attending school. He says he only went when it was raining and that he left at fourteen to join the Navy anyway. This is not strictly true, i.e. Grandpa has never been in the Navy. He left to work in a shuttlecock factory. But that is not the point. Will not be missing anything at school anyway as it is Sixth Form induction, i.e. wearing black, moaning about troops in Iraq, and listening to crap mix CDs.

4 p.m.

Hurrah. Plan has been utterly successful. Have spent day watching Jeremy Kyle and CBeebies with Baby Jesus and Grandpa (am not sure which is more disturbing— enraged women in lilac velour or *The Tweenies*). Plus have eaten proscribed Wagon Wheels, Monster Munch, and Bachelor's Supernoodles (Jesus's lunch of choice), which is excellent depression food. In fact, feel quite happy and energetic. It is all the sugar and Tartrazine. Grandpa says

13

the whole Justin/Sophie thing was inevitable and that all men are bastards who think with their willies. (Except for Dad. Who seemingly married Mum for her freakish ability to do logarithms in her head and get red wine stains out of cream shagpile.) Asked Grandpa if he had ever cheated on Grandma Riley. He said no. But not through choice. It is because Grandma Riley had arms the size of hams and a hive of killer bees. He does not need to cheat on Treena. Her demands for sex are insatiable. Grandpa says she will wear it out at this rate. At which point had to stop eating proscribed Peperami due to sausage/penis thing again.

Mum is not suspicious at all. She asked how school was and I just shrugged, i.e. not even a lie. She rolled her eyes and started on about teenagers being uncommunicative and that mobile phones and email are to blame and in her day she had to give a full account of the school day to Granny and Grandpa Clegg, including whether or not she had been to the loo and for what purpose. Luckily James stepped in to give his full account of school: fell off top of Keanu and Mad Harry in attempt to recreate pyramid of death, looked at some newts, learned theme from *Pet Rescue* on chime bars, went to loo twice—one poo, one wee. Primary school is a cinch. He will be in for a shock when he gets to John Major High. Although he will probably relish the challenge. Plus it is not at all certain he will go to John Major. He is still angling for boarding school. He says he is concerned state secondary

14

may not offer him the wide-ranging education he requires. It is because he wants to wear a cape and learn about Death Eaters. Have told him Hogwart's does not exist but he just smiled a knowing smile. He is an idiot.

Although it is possibly true about John Major High not being up to scratch. According to Scarlet, Sixth Form induction consisted of watching *Bowling for Columbine* in the audio-visual suite (i.e. hairy librarian Mr Knox's crap video machine). Mr Wilmott is trying to counteract any possible gun-toting activity. It is wishful thinking. The only gun-toting John Major High has ever witnessed is Mr Vaughan's crap splurge guns in *Bugsy Malone*. Although they did cause irreparable damage to the B Corridor ventilation shaft. Scarlet says I might as well not bother coming in all week as the anti-vice film theme is continuing tomorrow with some anti-drug vintage *Grange Hill*. Asked her if Justin mentioned me at all. She said he only managed to wrest his tongue out of Sophie's mouth long enough to eat a KitKat. It is gross. Public snogging is utterly undignified. Although was quite nice when he used to fling me against the lockers in fit of passion.

. . . .

Tuesday 17

It is nice at Grandpa's. There is no regime of fear regarding spillage, and the TV is on all day. So is kind of like the common room, but without the snogging, black clothing, and constant demands to sign petitions against whaling or war. Have got to give up the junk food though. Mum asked me if I had been sniffing glue when I got home. I pointed out that sniffing glue would make me spotty and lethargic, not buzzy and wild-eyed, but this did not seem to allay her fears. So admitted to eating a Wagon Wheel (to avoid menacing phone calls to Mr Wilmott) but cunningly said it was Sad Ed's. He is always eating so she will not suspect anything.

. . . .

Wednesday 18

Grandpa's is becoming a hotbed of truancy. I was not the only one watching *In The Night Garden* (drug-induced toddler programme involving weird maggot and some talking clothes pegs) and eating crisps on the faux leather sofa today. Unbelievably, Dad was also in attendance. I thought he was there to frogmarch me through the school gates, but it turns out that his boss Mr Wainwright had booked him on an Outward Bound team bonding course and Mum would not let him stay at home either. He says there is no way he is yomping around on the notoriously boggy fens with only Malcolm from IT to protect him. I do not blame him. Also he says CBeebies is possibly more educational than school. He is right. Today I learned how toothpaste is made, from a dog and a woman called Auntie Mabel who flies everywhere in a spotty plane. (Although may well write in to point out the carbon footprint implications.) Anyway, we have agreed not to grass each other up to Mum. Helped Dad smear some convincing mud on his Hush Puppies. Though he does not need my assistance. He has over twenty years' experience of avoiding Mum's Paxman-like questioning.

· ·

Thursday 19

8 a.m.

Dad is going to work today. I could see him struggling internally over his Oatibix between a day of crisps on the sofa or a day of arguing about the price of photocopier fluid, but he knows better than to push his truancy too far.

3 p.m.

Unlike me. The game is up. Mum knows everything. Her face (with menacingly thin lips) loomed at the window this afternoon just as Grandpa and I were settling down to *Diagnosis Murder*. Even Jesus screamed. I said it was utterly unfair and that Dad is a complete traitor as he had promised not to say anything. Which was my first, or possibly third or fourth, mistake, as it wasn't Dad who told her. Nor was it amateur private eye Marjory from next door with her binoculars and digital camera. Devastatingly, it was Sad Ed. (It turns out there was no Sixth Form at all today due to Criminal and Retard-related damage to the 'audio-visual suite' so he had come over to listen to

17

Morrissey CDs and moan about Tuesday.) Apparently he tried to run away, but his size is an impediment to speed, and Mum blocked him at the hydrangeas. Inevitably, he buckled under her interrogation. Which is crap, because I have taught him the rules several times, i.e. DO NOT look into her eyes. DO NOT admit to anything. If in doubt, have coughing fit or feign idiocy or death.

Mum is using her 'It is not me you are letting down, it is yourself' method of punishment. It is a lie. She thinks I am letting her down and will end up semi-literate like Granny and Grandpa Clegg. Have promised to go to school tomorrow, even though it is last day and will consist of idiotic Year Elevens spraying silly string over the mobile science labs and saying it is the end of an era etc., etc.

It is Dad I feel sorry for. There is no way he will be let off so easily. Mum is lying in wait for his return like the beast of Bodmin Moor. I did try to backtrack and claim that he was never actually at Grandpa's and that he had just rung and I answered the phone, but she said, 'Even you are not that stupid, Rachel.' Plus apparently Marjory has camera footage of him driving in the opposite direction to Wainwright and Hogg yesterday morning. She rang earlier to offer her services to track down the 'other woman'.

7 p.m.
Dad has confessed all. He tried to plead innocence with

the same 'I only rang' trick that I used but Mum said she was not an idiot (true) and showed him Marjory's incriminating footage. James says he is disappointed in both of us and that we have insulted his Ninja ways. He and Mum are watching Channel 4 news together on the sofa with an air of annoying self-satisfaction. Even the dog has a smirk on its hairy face. It is being allowed to sit in Dad's place. Its holier-than-thou attitude will not last. It is bound to have eaten, broken, or vomited up something by tomorrow.

8 p.m.
Or earlier. Dog banished to shed for barking frenzy at Jon Snow (who has replaced Natasha Kaplinsky as its most hated newsreader). Dad is back in his rightful place on sofa.

. . . .

Friday 20
8 a.m.
Today is the last day of school. Hurrah. Am not filled with nostalgia at all. In fact, like Gordon Brown, am looking firmly to future. From next term, will be actual Sixth Former and will no longer have to wear idiotic kilt and cardigan. Plus school will be free of morons like Mark Lambert, who is bound to let the sheep out, set off the fire alarms, and drink too much Tizer.

On down side, am going to have to face two-timing

rock legend Justin Statham and nipple pervert Sophie Microwave Muffins. Have texted Scarlet for reinforcements. She and Sad Ed are going to call for me on the way. I said Sad Ed has already proved his incompetence in these matters but she says he is reeling with remorse and has promised to shape up for future getaways.

4 p.m.
Am reprieved. Justin was not at school. Nor was Sophie Microwave Muffins. They were at Stansted airport with Mr and Mrs Microwave Muffins, waiting to fly to a villa in the Algarve. They are going for the whole summer. He has even quit his meat mincing for her. I hope they are going on easyJet. It is notoriously unreliable and the toilets are too small to do it in (according to Thin Kylie, who has tried several times). Was nice to have hench-men though. Jack came too to ensure I did not try to detour to Stansted to fling myself at Justin's mercy. I said hardly, as, in the absence of any of us owning a car, it involved getting on a smelly bus driven by Len Viceroy, followed by two separate and overpriced trains. (Although a teary airport reunion is utterly romantic. Will try to engineer one into my life at some point. If ever find love again.)

Last day of school entirely as predicted. C Corridor was strewn with funny (in no sense) foam, and the bodies of inconsolable Sixth Formers who think they will never see each other again. As if. They will all be back in Saffron

Walden in three years, living at home and having tedious conversations about how brilliant school was. Unlike me, Scarlet, and Sad Ed. As soon as we have got our degrees, we are moving to a bohemian squat in Camden and will return only to consume Christmas lunch.

On the plus side, Emily Reeve brought baby Lola Lambert in. She is coming back to school in September after all. Mrs Reeve is going to look after the baby. It is an excellent multi-generational solution. There is no way Mum would look after my baby if I got pregnant. She has enough trouble with Baby Jesus as it is. Mr Wilmott was visibly relieved. Not that he wants a teenage mum in the Lower Sixth, not even one who wears knee-length socks and pinafores. But it means his grade point average is safe again, following the announcement that one of the maths geeks is moving to Ipswich.

Plus Mark Lambert proved again that, contrary to expectations, he would make an excellent father. He selflessly dived across the foamy parquet to protect Lola from an oncoming sheep. Although apparently he was the one who let them all out in the first place. And set off the fire alarms and did Tizer sick in the language lab. I will miss him, despite his shaven head and moronic deeds. And the Kylies too. It will not be the same in registration without their endless supplies of *Heat* magazine, self-tan, and graphic details about Mr Whippy's 99. Oh, it is utterly the end of an era.

Saturday 21
7 a.m.

Ugh. Have got to haul self out of bed for day of toil at
lentil bins. Mum is refusing to phone in sick for me again.
Plus, have remembered that am still in debt to the tune
of several hundred pounds (Glastonbury, Dad's phone
bill, destruction of fake baby, etc.) so need all the money
I can get, even hunchback Mr Goldstein's paltry less-
than-minimum wages. On plus side Justin is no longer at
Goddard's, so will not be tempted to stare mournfully across
King Street at his bloodstained apron.

6 p.m.

Nuts In May particularly annoying. Sad Ed's mum, Mrs
Thomas, who works there in the week, had rearranged
the entire shop according to size and colour of packet
(going against Mum's preferred alphabetical system, and
against Mr Goldstein's preferred 'keep the tofu in the
fridge and the vitamins in one place' system) while Mr
Goldstein was at a yoghurt convention. He made me and
Jack spend all day putting things back where they belong.
Mrs Thomas will not last long if she keeps this behaviour
up. Mr Goldstein is very much not open to new ideas. I
bet he is rueing the day his last assistant, ailment-ridden
Rosamund, decided to run off with Guru Derek to his
yogic retreat in Steeple Bumpstead. At least she did what
she was told. Although she did have nits and eczema.

Jack was very understanding about me not wanting to

discuss Justin lest I wept too heavily over the linseed and made it germinate. He says the sooner I move on the better and asked if I wanted to go and see Rabid Hamsters play the ATC Hut tonight. Said no. The ATC Hut is too full of memories of Justin. Oh God. Have just realized that am never going to escape my tortured past. There is no other solution. Will ask Mum if we can move away. Preferably to London, where I can bond with fellow vintage-wearing and boy-hating prodigy Kate Nash.

8 p.m.
Mum says we are not moving away from Saffron Walden because, according to *The Times*, it is officially the best place to live in England. James backed her up with education, crime, and refuse collection statistics. His Google habit is getting out of control.

. . . .

Sunday 22
Granny Clegg has rung to remind us that she is having her hip of doom replaced by a nice, non-death-predicting metal one at the end of the week. I said she sounded remarkably happy, considering she was about to lose her special powers. She said, on the contrary, her bladder is playing up and she is hoping it is also blessed with the gift of second sight. Then she asked how I was and I told her about me and Justin. But instead of being sympathetic she got all excited as now she thinks the bladder can

divine relationship problems and she can make a fortune in matchmaking skills. That is the trouble with Cornwall. Unless you want to surf or eat Rick Stein pasties, there is precious little to do except imagine your body parts are psychic. Or marry a cousin. Oooh. Perhaps Granny and Grandpa Clegg are actually related. Have always had my suspicions. They do share the same swarthy looks and borderline racist tendencies. Will ask Mum.

4 p.m.
They are not related. Mum has already obtained authenticated birth certificate proof going back three generations.

Monday 23
Hurrah, it is the school holidays and have no homework or revision for once. Although do have lengthy booklist from Mr Knox for his AS level philosophy course. And several Shakespeares to plough through for English. In fact think have more work than ever before. At least am not James though. St Regina's does not break up until tomorrow for some reason, possibly to do with religion. Or INSET days. Or bloody-mindedness.

Normally at this point would be contemplating be-friending Thin Kylie to gain access to her kidney-shaped swimming pool, but it is unseasonally pouring with rain. Will go round Sad Ed's instead for some indoor moaning.

3 p.m.

Sad Ed is still utterly depressed about Tuesday. He says she is already sounding distant on their nightly phone calls. I said she was distant, i.e. 5,504 miles according to James. Sad Ed said it is not that. He thinks she is going to dump him for a tanned lifeguard with a six-pack called Chip or Brad, and he is contemplating moving his untimely death forward. I said how far forward. He said Thursday. I asked him what method he was thinking about and he said he is, as yet, undecided. So we went through the potential candidates. So far we have ruled out poison (impossible to procure without arousing suspicions of meddling shopkeepers); shooting (impossible to procure gun without becoming member of clay pigeon shooting club, which is beyond social acceptability); stabbing (too messy); drowning (Lord Butler pool lifeguards too enthusiastic, and shopping-trolley-clogged river Slade only two centimetres deep); and hanging (too clichéd). Pointed out that there are no methods actually left but Sad Ed is undeterred. He says he will find a way to join James Dean and Elvis as lost geniuses. He is deluded. Sad Ed will mostly be remembered for the time he fell off the climbing frame on the common and broke Emily Reeve's left leg. On plus side, endless discussion of death did not make me feel like joining Sad Ed in his quest, despite my current status as spurned lover. Scarlet says it is because I am out of Phase One post-break-up symptoms. Asked her what Phase Two is. She said inexplicable anger and man-hating. Am waiting its arrival eagerly.

. . . .

Tuesday 24

It is James's last day of school. He is delighted as it means he does not have to wear uniform. He has gone as a Ninja Turtle, predictably. Although it makes a change from his traditional outfits of choice—Virgin Mary or Smarties packet. Although the latter has been quarantined as Mum made it out of a giant cardboard tube from Carpet King and it turned out James couldn't actually walk in it and had to be rolled around the school. Besides, it would go soggy before he even got halfway down the road today, as it is still pouring with rain. What is point of summer holidays if not to lounge about garden reading *Vogue* and getting a tan (safely, of course, with factor fifty and a giant vintage sunhat)?

4 p.m.

James has come home from school with shocking St Regina's-related news. It is not anything to do with Keanu. (Although apparently he got sent home for dressing as a menacing hoodie. It was not fancy dress. It was daywear of choice.) It is that ancient and ineffectual headmaster Reverend Begley is retiring. Mum is delighted. She says things have gone downhill under his woeful lack of authority, and that now they might get a dynamic, go-getting superhead who will instigate a hothouse atmosphere replete with banks of computers and language labs, and exclude persistent bad influences like Keanu and possibly Mad Harry. She is going to be disappointed. It will probably be current Deputy Head Mrs Barrow who can barely control her Year Threes, let alone hardened Year Five criminals.

7 p.m.
Mum has sent Grandpa Riley into a panic with her St Regina's superhead predictions. It is because she told him it will put an end to the current 'take anyone gratefully' admissions policy and that Jesus will not get a place as he is officially in the catchment for R. A. Butler (aka Rag and Bone). Grandpa is booking Jesus in for a christening asap. I said I wasn't sure that it was legal to christen someone Jesus Harvey Nichols Riley but Dad pointed out that Auntie Joyless (severe Methodist relative in Cornwall) called her offspring Boaz Jehosephat and Mary Hepzibah, which is equally ludicrous. Then Grandpa got cross and said that there was nothing wrong with Jesus's name and if that was the way we felt then only the dog was invited. He is making a mistake. The dog is bound to jump in the font or eat the kneelers.

- -

Wednesday 25
Mum is in a Noah's Ark style panic. It is because flood waters have reached bastion of architectural and educational

supremity: Oxford. Previously she had been under impression that only Northern and unsavoury locations were in peril. She has gone to Homebase to buy sandbags. Have pointed out that we live on top of hill and that Slade is only body of water for several miles, unless you count Marjory's ornamental pond, but Mum is undeterred.

4 p.m.
Mum could be right about floods. According to James, Slade is now several inches under water, threatening to burst its banks and put the roundabout and 'slide of death' out of bounds. On plus side, it could be the answer to Sad Ed's suicide problems. Maybe God is listening after all. Will text him. Sad Ed, not God. Don't think God has a Nokia.

4.15 p.m.
Sad Ed has gone to inspect Slade to check its potential as scene of legendary untimely death.

7 p.m.
Sad Ed has confirmed that Slade is now four and a half inches deep and currently relatively shopping trolley free. He has asked me and Scarlet to meet him there tomorrow night at seven, i.e. before the Kylies arrive to do groping on the swings, and after tea. He does not want to drown on an empty stomach apparently.

Thursday 26

Today is a potentially momentous occasion, i.e. Sad Ed's untimely death. Obviously do not want him to die, but it has been his ambition since Year Seven so do not want him to be eternally disappointed in himself for not giving it a go. Besides, he is bound to fail, he is a notorious underachiever.

9 p.m.

Sad Ed still very much alive. But soggy and in bad mood. It is because he panicked when he put his head under water and saw several used condoms and a dead squirrel and changed his mind about the chosen location. But then he realized he was wedged in (Slade not being actual 'river' but more stagnant ditch) and had to be rescued by Mark Lambert's dad Mr Hosepipe (fireman, stripper, illegal mini-bike rider). It is his fault. I told him he should not have worn swimming goggles. If he had listened to me he would be dead by now. Instead he is facing potential harassment from Mark Lambert. And Mrs Thomas, when she sees what is stuck to his combat trousers. We are going to say he just overshot on the slide of death and fell in. That's what we told Mr Hosepipe. He says it happens all the time.

Friday 27

Granny Clegg goes into hospital today. She rang at 7.30 to say her last goodbyes. It is because she is convinced she is going to contract MRSA. She says Hester Trelowarren saw one when she was having her hysterectomy and it was green and the size of a Rolo. She is taking a multipack of wet wipes to combat them. Pointed out that if they are that big she will need more than a Johnson's wipe and that possibly a can of Raid would be in order. It was a joke but she has sent Grandpa Clegg to Spar to stock up.

Also Sad Ed is ill. It is because he swallowed some Slade water. He thinks it might be rabies. Asked what his symptoms were. He feels sick and has been to the toilet five times during *Hollyoaks*. Said he will live but if he starts foaming at mouth then to call NHS Direct. Oooh. Maybe would make excellent doctor. I could be like Dr Chris and diagnose menopausal things on daytime TV.

Saturday 28

Work was uneventful. There is nothing to do now that I cannot ogle Justin through the glucosamine window display. Even Jack was miserable. It is because he was on till duty, which is fraught with potential finger-trapping injuries. Went to commiserate with Sad Ed at lunchtime but he was not in his usual place, herding Waitrose trolleys round the multi-storey car park. Asked Mrs Noakes (no chin; bad perm; calls trousers 'slacks', formerly of WHSmith, now of Waitrose deli counter) where he might be located but she says he phoned in sick. She asked if I knew what exactly was wrong as he had been mysterious on phone and they are clamping down on sick leave ever since Gary Fletcher (former Criminal and Retard, sacked from pet food aisle for eating Bonio) phoned in with myxomatosis. I said it was not a fake sickness but was a very real failed suicide attempt. That shut her up.

Also Granny Clegg's hip replacement has been successful, i.e. hip of doom is out, new hip is in and there are no signs of marauding MRSAs on Sebastian Coe Ward as yet. She says she asked the surgeon if the hip had any mysterious markings on it. He has booked her an appointment with the psychiatric assessment unit. They must be busy in Cornwall. Half the population think they are druids.

Sunday 29

Went round to see Sad Ed this morning with Scarlet. He is still bed-ridden with Slade-induced stomach issues. Though it did not stop him consuming several bowls of Coco Pops during our visit. He says he needs the energy. What for? Reading *NME*? It is certainly not for pan-Atlantic phone sex as apparently Tuesday has not answered his last seven calls. He is preparing himself for the inevitable i.e. that he will be joining me and Scarlet in the ranks of singletons shortly. Am even more depressed as remembered it is my birthday in three days. Scarlet

31

suggested we have a party to perk ourselves up. She means play dirgy music and drink fake blood i.e. cider and blackcurrant. I said I am too depressed to dance, even to goth stuff. Plus there is no way Mum will let me have a party after last year's fiasco when Fat Kylie shaved the dog and the maths geeks did Bacardi-related vomit in the dining room. We are going to get drunk on a punt instead (if Sad Ed can raise himself from his sick bed). It is far more vintage and dignified.

7 p.m.
Oh God. Mum has just reminded me I have a dentist appointment tomorrow with sadistic Mrs Wong. I am having braces fitted, at the age of nearly sixteen. Is there no end to my woes?

Monday 30
Apparently not. Am utterly hideous. Have mouth full of metal and plastic. Am like Jaws in Dad's favourite crap James Bond film. Cannot speak without spitting at anyone within metre radius or sounding like have several speech impediments. Begged Mrs Wong to change her mind as tooth is only slightly wonky but she will not be moved. Plus she was armed with dangerous implements, and has a history of causing excess bleeding, so was too scared to argue. James has pointed out that I should be thankful I do not have to wear it at night. What is point

of that? Night is exactly when it is fine to wear it, i.e. when rest of world, and Justin Statham in particular, cannot see me. Am going to be laughing stock of common room. Will be forced to sit in 'Spaz' corner with the mathletes and Steve 'the scab' Britten, who has eczema.

Interestingly, though, Sad Ed's suicide bid was the hot topic in Mrs Wong's waiting room. Although the details appear to be a bit on the sketchy side. I overheard Mrs Dyer (unconvincing dye job, fat feet, smells of Yardley) telling Ying Brewster (child bride of Les, owner of Siam Smile Thai restaurant, formerly Dog and Bucket pub) that he swallowed five bottles of Calpol and tried to hang himself with his school tie in some sort of statement against conformity. Mrs Dyer said it is always the fat loners who go bonkers.

. . . .

Tuesday 31

The Sad Ed suicide rumours have reached new heights. Thin Kylie came over to ask if it was true he had tried to shoot himself with an assault rifle. She says it is all over the Whiteshot Estate (home of Grandpa Riley and several thousand O'Gradys). I said he was indeed recovering from suicide, but that no firearms were involved. She begged me to tell her the details but I said I am not a blabbermouth. Though someone is or these rumours would never have reached epic proportions. Then she demanded to know why I was 'talking like a mentalist'?

I showed her my brace. She said, 'You are, like, never going to pull with that. It could get caught on someone's knob.' Apparently Stacey O'Grady is still scarred from such an encounter.

Went round Sad Ed's to tell him the bad news about the suicide rumours but he says, *au contraire*, it is excellent as people think he is edgy and dangerous i.e. almost legendary. Although it will make his actual untimely death trickier as everyone will be watching him like a hawk now. I said I didn't think he should hold his breath. Anyway, he has made a Lazarus-like recovery and is definitely coming punting tomorrow, status of poos pending.

Also Granny Clegg has been given the all-clear by the hospital Psychiatric Assessment Unit, despite revealing all about the hip of doom, the bladder of love, and Jesus in the Nimble toast. Clearly she is just mildly mad compared to most of their cases.

august

Wednesday 1

Am sixteen. Which is, according to James, a milestone in my formative years as can now do several important things like have sex, buy cigarettes, and be gay without asking permission from Mum (in theory anyway, in reality will still be asking her permission to do 'It' when am thirty-six). And, according to MTV, should be getting ready for gigantic party complete with haute couture gown, hundreds of friends, semi-famous band, and fabulous boyfriend to snog. But, instead, am single, broke, and wearing speech-compromising braces. Not even birthday presents have cheered me up as did not get first edition Jane Austen or vintage Dior clutch bag asked for. Instead got National Trust membership (Mum and Dad); *Philosophy Made Easy* (James, in AS Level/Ninja anticipation); a giant tube of Fruit Pastilles (Granny and Grandpa Clegg, out of date); a Jordan's Porridge T-shirt, which I know for a fact came free with three coupons and a first class stamp (the dog, i.e. Mum); and *The Joy of Sex* (Baby Jesus, though assume purchased by Treena). It is my most disappointing haul yet. Mum has already quarantined the sex book to check it for age appropriateness. She is welcome to it. There is nothing joyful about excessively hairy people in compromising positions.

Plus it is raining so getting drunk in a punt has been ruled out in favour of sitting in Scarlet's den with some nibbles and Suzy's vast Eighties film collection. Scarlet was right. Am definitely in Phase Two of post-break-up trauma. No one could be angrier or more self-loathing than I am right now.

11 a.m.
Except Sad Ed. As predicted, Tuesday has dumped him. It is not for a tanned lifeguard called Brad or Chip, but for a cheerleader called Courtney. Apparently lesbianism is very in vogue in LA at the moment. Sad Ed is beside himself. He has bypassed Phase One self-pity and is already fully in Phase Two. We are going round Scarlet's immediately to find out what Phase Three is and when it will kick in.

11 p.m.
Scarlet says we should not even be thinking about Phase Three yet, as Phase Two could last for anything up to a year. But she has had an excellent idea. We are going to channel our anger into something positive and have made a mission statement for our plans. Our inaugural annual Rachel Riley birthday resolutions are as follows:

1. Not to moon about over exes but to embrace single life.
2. To stay away from all men. (Sad Ed excepted as he is not actual man. He tried to disagree on this but was outnumbered.)
3. To remain true to our friends, forsaking all others.
4. To remember that we alone are responsible for our own happiness.

Scarlet is right. Life will be so much easier without the complications of love. It will be utter Simple Life (in original meaning, not version involving anorexic American layabouts and rednecks) and am completely committed. Am starting tomorrow. Am going to do single-type activity, i.e. staying in bed late, eating copious chocolate, and reading self-help manuals.

. . . .

Thursday 2
8 a.m.
Plan slightly thwarted as got woken up at seven by dog falling down the stairs. And then Granny Clegg rang while I was trying to read *Philosophy Made Easy* (which is utterly self-improving as philosophers are too busy expanding their minds to think about sex) to tell us that there has been an emergency in St Slaughter—unpredicted by any of Granny Clegg's foretelling body parts. Grandpa Clegg's appendix has burst and he is two beds down from Granny on Sebastian Coe ward. Apparently he thought he had just eaten too much Fray Bentos so drank a glass of salt water (ridiculous ancient non-remedy) and instead ended up having emergency surgery. It is the nurses I feel sorry for. They are going to have a nightmare dealing with two Cleggs in one go. Mum has announced she is driving down tomorrow, as Granny Clegg is due out of hospital on Saturday and cannot be trusted to look after herself (Auntie Joyless

and religious cousins are at Bible Camp in Minehead willing stigmata on themselves or something). Granny Clegg said not to worry as her home help Hilary comes twice a week to do the heavy shopping and clean the loo and she can get Maureen from Spar to take Bruce (demonic offspring of dog) for a poo. But Mum says there is no way she is entrusting her own mother to a woman who thinks pasta is a vegetable (she means Maureen. Hilary is an unknown quantity, although, if past home helps are anything to go by, she has greasy hair, smokes, and drinks too much tea). She is leaving at dawn with James.

11 a.m.
Have had a genius idea. Where better to begin my new Simple Life than in Cornwall—county of nothing to do and where all men either chew straw or play the banjo. There will be utterly no temptation at all. Plus it will take my mind off GCSE results (due in three weeks and ringed in red on Mum's *Good Housekeeping* calendar in doom-laden way). I will be excellent home help to Granny Clegg and we can all bond across the generation gap. It will be like *Steel Magnolias* with me as brave and wise Julia Roberts, Mum as manic and paranoid Sally Field, and Granny Clegg as the mad one in dungarees. (Not sure who will be Dolly Parton though. Maureen wears overalls and has hair that defies any definition of style.) Am going to beg Mum to let me go.

40

1 p.m.

Hurrah. It is agreed. Am going to Cornwall tomorrow.
Asked Sad Ed if he wanted to come to take his mind off
the ghosts in Saffron Walden (metaphorical, not real.
Although Grandpa Riley claims he once saw a headless
horseman behind the Co-Op) and also his absence might
possibly fuel the suicide stories, but he has extra trolley
herding duty. Scarlet can't come either as she has to visit
her Aunt Sadie in Somerset who is a witch. (The Stones
are not having a summer holiday this year due to Suzy's
sex programme filming schedule. Apparently she is up to
her eyeballs in celebrity penises until September.) It is
utterly unfair. Scarlet has more than her fair quota of
interesting relatives i.e. sex guru mum, abortionist dad
etc., etc. All I have is accountants and a naval fantasist.
Anyway, it is a good thing, as she is going to do my
Saturday job for me. She is more acclimatized to all those
lentils, being a committed vegetarian.

. . . .

Friday 3

8 a.m.

Am wedged into Fiesta with four boxes of emergency
food (Mum does not trust Spar to stock wholewheat anything) and several sleeping bags (Granny Clegg's bedding
dates from 1950s and is perpetually damp). Am also in
priority position, i.e. front seat. Dad is not coming as
Mr Wainwright is on a cruise around the Baltics with

41

Mrs Wainwright Mark II and has left him in charge for two weeks. He is mad with power and has gone in already to impose his authority. The dog is not coming either. It is going into kennels. Mum says Dad cannot be trusted not to let it eat the furniture or otherwise maim or destroy the house. The journey is planned with military precision. We are due to arrive in St Slaughter at 2.20 exactly, with no stops whatsoever, not even for wees (it has been nil by mouth since 7 a.m.). There is also an absolutely no talking to the driver rule to avoid distraction and possible pile-up on the A303. I am listening to Sad Ed's iPod instead. He has lent it to me, to counteract endemic lack of edgy entertainment in the west country.

12 noon
iPod battery has run out. Thank God. No wonder Sad Ed is suicidal. Barely any of his music has a tune. Though did discover he has a Britney album. It must be some ironic thing.

2.20 p.m.
Mum is freakishly good at travel timings. She should be employed by Network Rail to redo their notoriously inaccurate timetable. Though her knuckles are white and hands bent into claw shape from gripping steering wheel so hard. We are going to unpack and then reconvene at 2.25 for a light lunch and chore allocation. (Belleview has deteriorated under Grandpa Clegg's management and

there is a layer of mould on all the windows. Possibly due to inclement weather. Or Bruce licking them.)

2.25 p.m.
James is late for Marmite sandwiches and chores, which is unlike him. He is like Mum when it comes to punctuality, and cleaning. Come to think of it, he has been strangely quiet all journey.

2.30 p.m.
James still absent. And have had worrying thought. Do not remember him actually being in car, i.e. there was complete lack of annoying singing or fact quoting or 'are we there yetting' from back seat.

2.35 p.m.
It has finally happened. James has triumphed and is 'Home Alone'! He must have taken advantage of Mum's panic at long-distance Fiesta driving to fulfil his Macaulay Culkin ambition. Mum is going mental with worry. She has rung the house several times but there is no answer. He is probably busy rigging a complicated trap involving pulleys, hammers, and buckets of paint across the hallway. Mum is going home immediately. I pointed out that Dad would be back in three hours to provide adult supervision but she says she might as well leave James in the care of the dog, if he is not dead already, or worse (what would this be?). She says she will be back tomorrow

43

with the escapee. Until then, I am under instructions to throw out all Fray Bentos, Viennetta, and tinned mandarins and fill fridge with health-giving food for Granny Clegg's recovery. She will go mental. She thinks hummus is the 'spit of the devil'.

10 p.m.
Mum has rung. James is safe after all. He had not rigged the house with man traps but instead had cleaned it thoroughly, including descaling the toilet, and was watching the History Channel with a bowl of Shreddies when Mum got in. There is something wrong with that boy. Although the dog had eaten two Bic biros (James had taken him out of kennels to act as his Ninja protector) and Dad had spilled an entire bottle of Jacob's Creek on the lino. On plus side, she has decided to leave me in charge of Granny Clegg, on grounds that her services are required more urgently in Saffron Walden (what with Dad being possible closet alcoholic). She has told me the secret location of Granny Clegg's savings jar (in the freezer, under the Aunt Bessie's Yorkshire puddings) for use in emergencies but in return I have had to agree to a long list of conditions, i.e:

- Do not let Bruce get in the bath with Granny Clegg;
- Do not let Bruce lick Granny Clegg's wounds;
- Do not let Granny Clegg persuade you to buy anything manufactured by Findus;
- Do not let Granny Clegg persuade you to buy

44

scratchcards, lottery tickets, or betting slips from 'Mad' Charley who races dogs illegally;

- Do not let Granny Clegg let Charley put Bruce into an illegal dog race or it will turn into an illegal dog fight.

11 p.m.
Granny Clegg is rich. She has amassed £273.57 in a Nescafé jar. Admittedly some of it is 'old' money (still currency in Cornwall probably), and I also noticed several chocolate coins, but none the less, it means we will be in practical lap of luxury. Am going to bed now. Though apparently Granny Clegg has been using spare room as general storage cupboard. Am wedged in between three ironing boards and an abdominiser.

1 a.m.
Cannot sleep. Leonard Cohen on iPod is tormenting me. Have realized it is first time have been in a house on own all night. What if burglars try to break in to steal the Cleggs' life savings? Am going to call Mum.

1.15 a.m.
James answered. He was up having a Ninja vigil with the dog. He told me to get a grip and that I am sixteen and need to demonstrate responsible adultness. Also, he pointed out that no one is going to break into a 1950s semi with filthy net curtains in search of treasure. This is true. Asked

about beast of Bodmin. He said to take garlic to bed as beasts of all kinds are notoriously afraid of garlic. Have got tub of hummus and wedged door shut with one of ironing boards as extra precaution.

. . . .

Saturday 4

8 a.m.

Have cleared out spare room in spring clean frenzy after ironing board fell on head in night and thought it was marauding burglar. Have thrown out boards, abdominizer, and ten hamster cages. Since when has Granny Clegg ever had a hamster? Let alone ten? On plus side, have found two utterly vintage dresses in a Spar bag. Have put them in wash and will wear them in manner of Fifties starlet on healthy Riviera holiday. Though is still raining outside so will have to wear wellies instead of peep-toe kitten heels.

Also have just spoken to Granny Clegg. They are bringing her home at two o'clock in an ambulance. She is very excited as she thinks it is going to be like on *Holby City* with sirens going and pedestrians flinging themselves to the pavement to get out of the way. She is going to be disappointed. Have also spoken to Maureen Penrice who is currently in charge of canine menace Bruce. She is bringing him back at two as well and says it cannot come soon enough. He has terrorized her Alsatian Arnie ceaselessly, as well as eaten a signed photo of Phillip Schofield.

3 p.m.
Granny Clegg is home. She got carried over the threshold by a beardy paramedic called Dave. She says she can die happy now. In contrast Bruce got thrown over threshold by Maureen who claimed Granny owed her £10 for dry cleaning after Bruce ate an entire jar of pickled cabbage and threw it up on her best skirt. Paid her out of the emergency jar, even though I know for a fact all her clothes are machine washable polyester and she will just spend the money on astrology magazines. Anyway, Granny and Bruce are both recovering on the flock-patterned sofa, eating barley sugar and watching the snooker. Told Granny I did not think boiled sweets were good for Bruce's teeth. She says he swallows them whole so it doesn't matter. I did not like the look Bruce gave me at that point. He is plotting against me. I can tell.

5 p.m.
Granny Clegg's occupational therapist Karl (long hair, earring, smell of patchouli) has been to check that conditions at 'Belleview' are suitable for convalescing ancient person. Conclusion—no, but he'll bring a special loo seat along in a few days when Mr Patterson on Petroc Street has finished with it. Am under strict instructions not to let Granny do any lifting/carrying or unwarranted walking at all. This is not difficult as she avoids all three as matter of course anyway.

7 p.m.
Have made honey-cured organic Wiltshire ham sandwiches for tea (told Granny Clegg it was limited edition
Spam). She has gone to bed already. She says all the
painkilling drugs she is on make her sleepy. She does not
mind; apparently they give her 'unmentionable dreams'.
It does not bear thinking about. I, on other hand, am
going for a reviving country walk with Bruce. Scarlet was
right. The simple life is utterly rewarding and do not need
boyfriend at all when have literary ponderings and faithful companion.

9 p.m.
Country walk not quite as reviving as hoped as actual
'country' is impenetrable moorland, rife with giant black
cats and potential murderous ex-tin miners, so wandered
aimlessly around only Rec, avoiding stares from bog-eyed
youths.

Sunday 5
Granny Clegg is demanding to be taken to church. I
pointed out she had not been since 1994, due to
installation of 'new-fangled' woman vicar but she says her
new hip is making her do strange things. She thinks it may
be infested with the soul of whomever it came out of. I said
it was not a transplant hip but a man-made metal one but
she is not convinced and has told me to put my Sunday

48

best on. Am wearing vintage Fifties thing with giant hole in seam but have safety-pinned it up so knickers do not show. On plus side, maybe will have revelation, i.e. God will appear to me above the font and I will repent all my sins and become a nun. It would help with the swearing off boys thing and is the ultimate Simple Life.

10 a.m.
Granny Clegg says her sister Carol died wearing safety-pinned Fifties dress. She got run over by a meat lorry. The hole is where they cut her out of it.

1 p.m.
Granny Clegg has decided she does not like church after all as it smells funny. Which is rich coming from someone whose entire house is impregnated with odour of processed meat and foot powder. I on other hand have had total church-based revelation! Have not become nun *but* during sermon (something to do with pillars of salt—possibly anti-heart disease theme) spotted utterly gorgeous boy three pews in front, i.e. was not wearing Kappa tracksuit, chewing straw, or in possession of extra limbs. He was tall, with normal complement of arms and legs, and wearing vintage Levi's. And he is black. Am going to track him down and befriend him. Oooh. We could get married and incur wrath of middle-class anti-mixed race marriage masses. Hurrah. Mum will go bonkers.

2 p.m.

Though obviously am totally off men so will just be
platonic exotic friend. Though have removed brace and
stored in Players tobacco tin on windowsill. Do not want
to spit on anyone. Platonic or otherwise.

5 p.m.

Have lurked around all usual 'youth' spots (cigarette
counter at Spar, fruit machines in Bubbles Launderette,
disused playground) but to no avail. He is nowhere to be
found. Maybe he was apparition. Or, more probably, does
not actually live in St Slaughter as it is utterly backward.

Monday 6

Granny Clegg says she is going on hunger strike if she has
to eat any more of Mum's multigrain wholemeal batch.
She says in her condition being bunged up would be a
blessing as negotiating the loo is particularly tricky (I can
bear witness to this after she made me 'ease' her on to the
seat five times yesterday). She sent me to Spar for a loaf of
Nimble and a tin of Pedigree Chum (Bruce is also on strike
and will not eat Mum's health-giving vegetable-based dried
dog biscuits). Went to disused playground to call Sad Ed
(Granny has banned me from using her phone in case I call
a sex line or America) and tell him about church boy. He
said I should not be thinking about men at this crucial
point in Phase Two and reminded me of our pact. I said,

au contraire, I was hoping to secure him as my new best male friend i.e. utterly platonic and with no sex thoughts of any kind. Sad Ed said what about him but I said I don't fancy him, so there is no challenge. Then the line got crackly and I got cut off. The signal in Cornwall is hopeless. How anyone gets anything done is beyond me. Anyway have still not located church boy so plight is pointless.

5 p.m.
Grandpa Clegg has rung to demand to be discharged. He says the nurses are possibly in league with giant pharmaceutical companies (he actually said farmacuticle) and are plotting to use him for human vivisection experiments. Plus they keep trying to look at his 'widgie'. He is worse fantasist than Grandpa Riley. Pretended line was bad, then hung up. Mum would be proud.

Tuesday 7
10 a.m.
Oh my God. An unbelievable thing has happened. Utterly gorgeous boy from church is home help Hilary! In fact, is at this very moment making Ovaltine to Granny's secret recipe (i.e. double the Ovaltine and evaporated milk). Am in shock as cannot believe Grandpa Clegg would allow anyone black over threshold. Particularly with a girl's name. Am going to investigate immediately. Once have put on vintage Fifties dress, which says 'am interesting

worldly-wise Kate Nash-type', as opposed to Jordan's Porridge T-shirt, which says 'I eat cereal and am type of nerd who sends away for freebie T-shirts'.

11 a.m.
Have secured following information from Granny Clegg re 'Hilary':

- He comes twice a week, on Tuesdays and Fridays;
- He is son of Granny's favourite Welsh dentist Mr Nuamah.
- He is named after someone in the Labour Party (a man), which bodes well as parents are obviously progressive, as opposed to inbred jingoists like most of St Slaughter.
- This is a holiday job. Normally he is doing A levels and is going to be a doctor 'when he grows up', i.e. he is both clever and selfless.
- Grandpa Clegg tried to object to his presence but council said it was that or he could do his own shopping (Grandpa Clegg does not do shopping as it is woman's work). He is now of opinion that it is like being rich plantation owner and having servant.
- They refer to him as 'Chalky'. (Or at least Grandpa Clegg does. Granny Clegg uses her favoured method of silently mouthing words she is embarrassed by, with the helpful addition of sign language. Like 'gay' (limp wrist). Or 'black' (point at face). Or 'Ann Robinson' (wink menacingly).)

This is outrageous. Am going to offer to join him in protest against racist employers. Even if they are relatives.

12 noon
Have had groundbreaking conversation with Hilary along following lines:

Me: I'm utterly sorry that my non-multicultural grandparents call you 'Chalky'. They are a bit, um, backward.

Hilary: It's not their fault. They are of a generation that was brought up under the malign Conservative influences of Enoch Powell. Their ignorance will die with them.

Me: Totally. They are institutionally racist. It's embarrassing. Do you want a can of Lilt?

Hilary: No thanks. I am allergic to pineapples.

Me: How ironic.

Hilary: Why?

Me: Um. I just . . .

Hilary: Yeah. Whatever. And in case you were wondering, I can't dance and my penis is of average size.

Me: Right. Uh. Do want a cup of tea?

Hilary: One sugar, please.

As if I was wondering about his penis. Am still scarred by the whole 'Donkey' Dawson/Duchy Originals pork sausage thing. Plus am utterly progressive and know it is outdated media stereotype. Anyway, Hilary is utterly modern and I think love him (platonically) even more. Cannot believe have to wait three days until I see him again.

· ·

Wednesday 8

Interrogated Granny Clegg for more information about the Nuamahs so that I can bond with Hilary on several levels. Results as follows:

- Mr Nuamah does not eat garlic (this is plus point for the Cleggs, who are also garlic-fearers, though in their case it is because it is 'foreign muck' and, in Mr Nuamah's case, it is because he does not want toxic breath on his patients).
- They live in St Enodoc's (aka the 'big house' off the B3298).
- Mrs Nuamah does not shop in Spar, much to Maureen Penrice's relief, who thinks they will have trouble understanding her, being 'of foreign extraction'. (It is possibly true, though more to do with Maureen's unfathomable accent and use of word 'hooge'.)
- Mrs Nuamah does shop in M&S in Truro, according to Hester Trelowarren, who spotted her with a basket full of mini Jaffa Cake bites.

There is not much to go on. Though at least I know where he lives. And his preferences, snack-wise.

11 a.m.
Not that am going to stalk him.

1 p.m.
Have eaten lunch (Waitrose lemon sole goujons, aka 'Spar scampi'). May just go for bracing country walk with Bruce.

3 p.m.
Have abandoned country walk as traffic on B3298 is absurd. Have been honked at by 4x4s almost perpetually. Bruce is traumatized. Plus rain showing no signs of abating and vintage dress is too leaky due to car crash holes. Will just have to wait until Friday to see Hilary.

3.30 p.m.
Not that that was why was walking. Obviously. Was just exercising body and mind. In region of St Enodoc's.

• •

Thursday 9
Still raining.

Mum has rung to check that Granny Clegg is recovering nicely i.e. am I managing to slip health-giving foods into her somehow. I said I had got her to eat blueberries (American, and, therefore, untrustworthy) and fromage frais (French, see above) by calling it trifle, and frozen soya beans (too many issues to list), by claiming they were giant magic peas. She said it all tasted funny but I said it was the after effects of general anaesthetic making everything a bit sour. Asked how things were at home. She said James is trying to invent powerless flight, Dad sacked Malcolm for challenging his new filing system (but reinstated him when computers crashed and no one else knew what to do), and Marjory thinks the Britchers might be aliens (strobing lights, strange noises). I said they are not aliens, it is Terry testing out his new mobile disco. Or possibly Cherie's sunbed is on the blink. Asked if anyone had rung for me. She said if by anyone I meant Justin then no. I said no, by anyone, I mean anyone. She said no. Although she did bump into Mr Goldstein renewing his car tax (Fiat Multipla) at the post office and he asked when I was coming back as apparently Scarlet is not as au fait with the whole lentil thing as I thought and has demanded that he ban several non-vegetarian-friendly gelatine-based vitamin supplements. Plus she does not abide by the 'hour' bit of lunch hour.

Also, the hospital rang to remind us to fetch Grandpa from Sebastian Coe ward tomorrow as he is being discharged, ready or not. I said it was shocking that old people have to leave hospital when they are still incapacitated, just to free up beds. The nurse said Grandpa Clegg is not incapacitated. *Au contraire*, they are sick and tired of him ranting that Gordon Brown is plotting to wipe out law-abiding *Daily Mail* readers with his chemical weapon of choice, MRSA. Apparently he has been whipping all the old people up into an anti-NHS frenzy. As the ringleader, he is out first.

But it is good news because Hilary is going to drive us there to collect him in his environmentally friendly Nissan Micra. Will barely sleep with excitement. (And also because Granny Clegg sleepwalks. Last night she came in at two to tell me to 'put the bins out, Norman'.)

Friday 10
Still raining.

9 a.m.
Am ready to collect Grandpa and feeling utterly Florence Nightingaleish. Am going to impress caring Hilary with my progressive ability to also overlook racism and rantings of all sorts. Plus am wearing swirly vintage Monsoon dress, as borrowed off sex guru Suzy. It is almost ethnic.

5 p.m.
Grandpa Clegg is home and restored to his seat of power, i.e. the broken Parker Knoll. He says he is never going back into hospital, not even if he gets smallpox or TB (the Cleggs are not immunized, in case it was a plot by Harold Macmillan to wipe out the working classes). According to Grandpa, even the food is dangerous and left-wing. He cited Moroccan chicken, Russian salad, and lentil soup

as among the chief offenders. He got a cheer from all the other old people when he left. He is their anti-establishment hero. It is a sad day. He is about as far from Martin Luther King as you can get.

But am choosing to follow Hilary's lead and be zen-like in face of ignorance. He is studying Buddhism as part of his A Level religious studies. Was worried he might be planning on being priest i.e. utterly non-sexual and possibly gay, but it turns out he took it to feed his metaphysical side. I said that was exactly why I was doing AS philosophy. He said, 'Right. You're doing Chem, Physics, Bio, and maths too, huh.' Luckily at that point a sheep wandered into the road and he had to swerve the Nissan Micra so got away with a sort of mumble. Anyway, he is applying to Cambridge to study medicine next year. Hurrah. So I will be able to take tea with him in his Quad (no idea what this is but it sounds exciting) and show him ancient East Anglian traditions like pargetting and minibike racing.

6 p.m.
Hurrah. Grandpa Clegg has burst his stitches from getting shouty about some Polish plasterers on page four of the *Mail*. Hilary is taking him back to A&E. I begged to go too, but Granny Clegg said I had better watch Bruce as he is prone to self-harming if he is left alone for too long. Apparently he chews his legs. Which, in my opinion, is better than chewing everyone else's legs, which is his

activity of choice at the moment. At least I got to watch Hilary manhandle Grandpa into the back seat. He has very defined biceps.

8 p.m.
Grandpa Clegg is back amongst his minions on Sebastian Coe ward. Apparently the nurses are not happy, but A&E said his ranting was disturbing the trauma victims and he was better off with his own. He has begged Granny Clegg to bring him in a week's supply of Spar pink wafers to keep his strength up. Hilary is taking him a batch tomorrow, along with a three-pack of anti-MRSA babywipes. Granny says she definitely saw one scuttle under the communal commode.

. . . .

Saturday 11
Raining. When will this inclement weather cease? It is playing havoc with my wardrobe. Plus hair is back in giant puffball mode.

Rang Scarlet to check how she was progressing at Nuts In May but Jack answered. He said wholefood retailing is not the same without me. Apparently Scarlet is refusing to do till duty on grounds of Health and Safety and has threatened to call inspectors in. Mr Goldstein is thinking of sacking her.

Also, iPod has gone suspiciously missing (bad) along with my brace (good). Granny says it might be the Bermuda

Triangle in the scullery, as she is always leaving sliced meats in there and they disappear within minutes. She is deluded. It is not a Bermuda Triangle. It is Bruce. He is eyeing me with a look of smug self-satisfaction. So am now forced to listen to Granny's Burl Ives records plus owe Sad Ed £129. Am like impoverished third world country, i.e. destined to be for ever in debt. Though at least am not facially disfigured any more.

. . . .

Sunday 12

8 a.m.

Not raining. Hurrah. Am going to seize moment to go to Spar on Sunday papers errand as paper 'boy' Reggie Shovel (73, anorak, trousers too short) is off sick with shingles. I said I may well write to Gordon Brown to complain about pitiful state of pensions and old people being forced into menial and undignified labour but Granny Clegg says he does it for the exercise and free *Sun*.

9 a.m.

Raining. Sun was brief blip in otherwise continuous drizzle. Granny Clegg is annoyed because the paper is soggy (used it to protect inflating hair) and she is being forced to read my *Vogue* (shiny, so water-resistant), until the *News of the World* dries out on the bar heater. Am also

60

hovering near bar heater as need to be dry for church at eleven. Granny Clegg says I am wasting my time as God only likes puritanical mentalists like Auntie Joyless (she actually said mentalist). I said I was just going out of philosophical interest. That shut her up. She thinks philosophy is bordering on witchcraft. Have also rung James to get loads of Kofi Annan facts to impress Mr Nuamah (they are from same village in Ghana). For example, he is married to a Swedish lawyer and his name means a boy born on a Friday.

9.15 a.m.
Have had genius idea. Am going to dreadlock hair. It will prevent any more moisture-based issues and is utterly non-racist!

10.15 a.m.
Am dreadlocked. Ish. Is a bit messy and dreads are inch-thick in places, but is excellent none the less. Granny Clegg says I look like I have not washed in weeks. Hurrah.

12 noon
Mr and Mrs Nuamah were not in church. Nor was Hilary. Thought they might have been called out on a dental emergency. But apparently (according to Maureen's sister Barbara, who sits two pews down to the left) they have gone shopping in Plymouth. So my

Kofi Annan facts have been utterly wasted. Tried to creep out during 'For Those in Peril on the Sea' but the lady vicar thought I was offering myself up for communion. So now am awaiting wrath of Lord for eating wafery thing and drinking vile wine (Co-Op own brand, I saw a case under the altar) when am not actually even baptized.

2 p.m.
Mobile phone has gone missing. Granny is blaming scullery Bermuda Triangle. Normally I would blame Bruce but think it might be God.

4 p.m.
No, was Bruce. Have found it buried with iPod, brace, and a pair of aertex pants in his lair (i.e. the cupboard under the stairs). The number nine key is missing so will not be able to do any emergency calling, or texting involving the letters WXY and Z. On plus side iPod looks relatively unscathed so do not owe Sad Ed anything. Will say chew marks are acceptable wear and tear and he should have insurance for such eventualities. Also brace is beyond use. Hurrah.

5 p.m.
iPod worse than I thought. Memory has wiped all but two songs. 'Hit Me Baby One More Time' (Britney) and 'I'd Do Anything' (West End cast recording of *Oliver*).

9 p.m.
Have given iPod back to Bruce. Cannot listen to stage school brats offering to lace my shoe again or may well have to join Sad Ed in his quest for untimely death.

· ·

Monday 13
Raining.

Am bored. And I know I should be bonding with Granny Clegg across the generations and listening to her tales of Cornish yesteryear, but her memory is cloudy and she just keeps going on about Eamonn Holmes, who is neither Cornish nor historic. Thank God Hilary is coming tomorrow. We have so many things in common, i.e. we are both outcasts in Cornish society, and we both like philosophical things. Plus my hair is bordering on the Afro. Although may have to undread it soon as it is getting a bit itchy.

· ·

Tuesday 14
Oh my God. Granny Clegg is a pawn in a giant Cornish drug ring! Hilary and I were clearing the vegetable patch at the back and have discovered marijuana plants! Actually I thought it was smelly sycamore shoots but Hilary is more worldly wise in these matters. He says we should call the police immediately, as someone is obviously infiltrating her runner bean frames and using it as an illegal narcotics

63

factory. We are awaiting arrival of PC Penrice (brother of Maureen and Barbara). Once he has moved Hester's chickens out of Smeg Launderette. That is the downside of free-range poultry. They have no sense of territory.

Also have undreaded hair. Hilary says it makes me look like a trustafarian. Which is not at all progressive or left-wing. I think.

2 p.m.
Oh my God. Granny is not a pawn. She is the drug baron! She cracked under interrogation by PC Penrice and confessed that she got it off 'Crazy' McCaffety's pot plant (how ironic) stall at the Illogan fete and has since been handing it out to several youths in the area. She insisted that it is just some sort of herb and they are using it in casseroles but PC Penrice was not fooled and asked her to 'accompany him to the station for further questioning'. Hilary was brilliant and demanded her right to legal representation but Granny Clegg says she doesn't trust lawyers (she has been watching too much *Judge John Deed*) and could she take Hester from over the road instead. Hilary has called his mum anyway. She is a solicitor in Truro and is bound to be used to police brutality/accused stupidity etc. Hilary and I are going to wait it out at Belleview. Mainly because other-wise half the house will disappear into Bruce's Bermuda Triangle. May do some worried sobbing. Then Hilary will take pity on me and comfort me in his manly arms.

7 p.m.
Granny Clegg has been released without charge. She is disappointed as she was hoping for a night in the cells. She says it is very nice in there and people brought her PG Tips every half hour and a Bird's Eye Steak Grill for tea. Felt a bit guilty and put kettle on immediately. Anyway, apparently Mrs Nuamah befuddled the police with technicalities like the fact that Granny wasn't actually selling it and thought it was some sort of oregano. Asked what Hester's contribution was. Granny said she was in charge of doling out Fox's Glacier Mints.

Anyway, the drugs have gone. Two men in suits came and dug them up during *Blue Peter*. Hilary says they are Narcs i.e. plain clothes anti-drugs policemen. It is a shame really as it would have been edgy to have a dope-smoking granny. But something good has come out of it all i.e. Hilary gave my arm a squeeze when I got a bit tearful (actual genuine tears, though caused by Bruce biting my foot, not incarcerated Granny) so he definitely likes me.

7.15 p.m.
In a platonic way, of course.

7.30 p.m.
Although it would be nice if it was in an 'I fancy you and quite want to fiddle with your admittedly only 32A bra' kind of way.

Wednesday 15

Mum rang to check up again. Have not told her about the drugs shame. She would panic and despatch Dad to remove me from Granny's den of vice. Just told her that Hilary and I were managing to cope with every eventuality. Mum said Hilary sounds like a real find. I said 'mmm' in non-committal manner. Do not want to arouse suspicion. Luckily she changed subject to James and Mad Harry who have taken to dressing in leotards and tights. I said it is excellent that they are expressing their feminine sides. She said it is not feminine sides. It is some sort of Ninja wear and they have been terrorizing Marjory with their mysterious dancing in the garden.

Have made Granny twenty-two cups of tea to make up for previous lax attitude. She has begged me to stop as her bladder is 'like Niagara falls'. There is no pleasing some people.

. . . .

Thursday 16

Took Bruce to disused playground on pretext of a poo trip but actually to ring Sad Ed. He is depressed again. I said is it the metaphorical ghosts but he said no it is the extra trolley duty and it is causing him to lose will to live. I said I thought he had lost it years ago i.e. his untimely death ambitions. He says that was motivated by a desire to be legendary, his current suicidal tendencies are motivated by a desire not to have to listen to Gary Fletcher talk about remote-controlled cars for eight hours a day. I said at least it is keeping his mind off women but he said Gary Fletcher keeps talking breasts as well. Then he asked how I was holding up with my platonic pact. I said that at no point had I tried to snog or otherwise manhandle Hilary (which is utterly true), and that I am more committed than ever to the Simple Life. (Which is sort of true.)

8 p.m.
But what if it turns out that, in fact, Hilary is my ONE? It is possible. There is a definite frisson in the air when we are in the room together.

8.30 p.m.
No. Am not going to break my pact on the grounds of a frisson. Anyway, it is probably just the static off Granny's nylon carpet.

9 p.m.
But on other hand, one cannot mess with fate. Will lure him into potential snog situation and leave the gods to do their work.

. . . .

Friday 17
2 p.m.
I have a date with Hilary! Well, not a date exactly, but an assignation none the less. He is taking me to his Labour

Party constituency meeting tonight. I said I was a seasoned party campaigner (vaguely true, e.g. Jack's mock election campaign. Plus am always opposing social injustices, e.g. Mrs Brain's povvy table etc.) and would love to see how the grassroots supporters were holding up in the LibDem heartlands (I heard this on Radio 4 once). He said good, as they were debating the reinstatement of Clause 4 and would value my opinion. Am going to call Jack to find out what this means immediately.

7 p.m.
Aaagh. Jack's number has been deleted off my contacts by malign forces, i.e. Bruce, and I can't call it in normal way as it involves a nine. Am going to have to improvise. Have told Granny Clegg I am going to hang out at the bus shelter. She will panic if she thinks I am 'in cahoots with commies'.

10 p.m.
Nothing happened. The back room of the Farmer's Arms was obviously not sexually charged enough. It was all the sensible footwear. Plus I think I may have got Clause 4 confused with Section something else as I said it was outrageous they were even thinking about reinstating blatant anti-homosexual laws and I would voice my opposition all the way to Number 10. Why am I not doing A Level politics? In fact, may drop French and swap. It is a dead language after all and politics is international in its

influence. On plus side, we are meeting tomorrow. He is going to show me his signed photo of someone called Barack Obama.

. . . .

Saturday 18

2 p.m.

Fate was conspicuous by her absence from St Enodoc's this afternoon i.e. nothing happened again. Maybe it is like Phil and Kirstie say, i.e. location, location, location. The pictures of Tony Blair looming down at us from his bedroom walls did not help. Nor did Mr Nuamah who offered to fix my 'dental misalignment'. Did not mention the missing brace. He will be wiring me up with 24-hour metalwork within minutes.

Am definitely taking up A Level politics though. Hilary showed me his photo and I said it was nice to see basketball players in suits for once instead of all that Lycra. It turns out Barack Obama is running for President in America. How was I to know that? He is way too good-looking for a politician. Where is the helmet hairdo? Where are the bad teeth?

And got devastating news when I got back to Belleview. Dad is coming on Monday to repatriate me to North Essex. It is because Mr Wainwright is back from his cruise and is reasserting his authority, much to Dad's disappointment. Also Auntie Joyless is back from Bible camp today and will no doubt reinstate herself as chief Clegg tea maker. So am now in last-chance saloon as far

69

as the gods and Hilary go. And that saloon is St Slaughter Church. So gods will be in abundance at least.

5 p.m.
Rang Scarlet to tell her about my new uber-left-wing friend. She is very keen to meet him. Platonically, obviously. I said I would invite him to Saffron Walden as soon as possible. Then she said that she had news too. Apparently it is ultra secret and mindblowing and she will tell me about it when I get home. I said tell me now but she said it was possibly illegal and Suzy thinks the phones have been bugged by rival TV networks so it is face-to-face information only. (Wish I had not blabbed on about Granny being drugs baron now. ITV will be ringing her up to be on *Jeremy Kyle* any minute.) Oh God. Hope Suzy has not been giving her valium again.

Also she has been sacked. It is for 'persistent contrariness'. And lateness. Apparently she did not go in until half eleven today. I said was it because her biorhythms were wrong but she said no it was because *Friends* was on T4 and it was the one where Joey gets his eyebrows plucked. Anyway Scarlet says she does not care because money is not important in the grand scheme of things. This is easy to say when your mother is a primetime TV star and does not believe in withholding hereditary wealth and ferociously instilling work ethic. In other words Scarlet does not have to clean up cat poo to earn her pocket money.

Sunday 19

9 a.m.

This is it. It is D-Day for establishing whether Hilary and I are meant to be platonic or underwear-touching friends. Hopefully he will be fired up by the presence of higher beings and fling me romantically across the vestry. Am wearing miniskirt and ironic Mickey Mouse T-shirt (age 8). Which is not very religious but makes bust look bigger and gives air of potential availability.

2 p.m.

Aaagh. Have been thwarted by gods. Or rather by Auntie Joyless. Who has a power beyond any divine being. She and my god-bothering cousins got back from Bible camp last night and Granny Clegg happily informed them I had 'seen the light' and had 'gone all Gloria Hunniford'. So at ten o'clock she packed me in the back of her Mini Metro with Boaz and Mary and took me to get baptized at her evangelical Methodist Mission at the back of Somerfield in Redruth. So am now soaked to skin having been dipped in underfloor paddling pool by someone called Father Abraham (incomprehensible accent, gigantic sideburns, haunted look of *Crimewatch* photofit). Plus am probably harbouring legionnaires' disease. That pool was on the utterly murky side. And had to listen to drippy Mary going on about how Jesus was her best friend. Cannot believe am related to these morons. If Jesus wants any of them as a sunbeam he is mad.

Am going round Hilary's immediately. Once have taken off wet smock. (Auntie Joyless would not let me get baptized looking like the 'whore of Babylon'.)

7 p.m.
The gods have made their intentions known. Hilary and I are destined to be no more than friends. It turns out that he has a girlfriend. She is called Paloma and is half Spanish, i.e. also an ethnic minority. He was round her house in Truro when I called for him. According to Mrs Nuamah, who answered the door, they have been together ever since they met in chess club in Year Eight.

It is inevitable. I am not multicultural enough for him. Why oh why am I not browner? It is utterly unfair and potentially racist. It is not my fault I was born so pale. I blame Mum. The Cleggs have definite ginger tendencies.

It is probably for the best though. As Scarlet pointed out, it is important that we learn to love ourselves before we can expect anyone else to love us. Sad Ed will be waiting for ever. He is filled with self-loathing.

• •

Monday 20
The hospital has rung. Grandpa Clegg is being discharged again. Asked Granny if Hilary was going to get him but she said Dad will be here by two and he can get him in the Passat. Then she asked why I was so miserable. I said it was

potential legionnaires' disease from the religious paddling pool. She said I am lucky, apparently Auntie Joyless's friend Vivian was in hospital for months after being submerged last year, as predicted by the hip of doom. (Although on further interrogation it turns out she fell down a manhole and hospitalization was not exactly pool-related.)

3 p.m.
Dad has arrived. Asked him where James was, as I assumed he would have come along for the ride, but apparently he is too busy with his Ninja dancing. Plus Dad says he cannot endure twelve hours of him singing the Turtles theme tune. He has taken Granny Clegg to fetch Grandpa. I am watching Bruce to ensure Dad's wallet does not disappear into the Bermuda Triangle. Ooh. Knock at door. Is probably local type trying to procure oregano. Four have called already. Have sent them to see Crazy McCafferty, i.e. the evil overlord.

4 p.m.
Was not mental Cornish drug fiend. It was Hilary. He came to say goodbye! He has promised to visit me in Saffron Walden when he comes up for his Cambridge interview and I have promised to keep the red flag flying. We have swapped phone numbers and are now utterly best friends. He left just as Grandpa and his entourage got back from the hospital. Dad asked who the 'young negro' was (he is trying to be non-racist but, as usual, it backfires

horribly). Grandpa (who is trying to be racist) said, 'That's the houseboy, Chalky.'

Tuesday 21

Am home. In non-multicultural Saffron Walden. Predictably Mum is in spasms about Hilary. She says it is not that he is black, it is that he is a man, and may try to take advantage of Granny Clegg. It is that he is black. There is no way anyone would try to take advantage of Granny Clegg. Not even Grandpa Clegg. I warned Dad this would happen, but he said if he didn't tell her she would wheedle it out of him, and then make him pay for not coming clean in the first place. He is right. She is merciless.

On plus side, James has offered to restore my mobile phone to working capacity. He claims his Ninja powers have given him healing hands. Plus he has a vast collection of electrical things and probably has a spare nine key somewhere.

4 p.m.

Phone is restored. Though nine key is pink and gigantic. Have texted Scarlet to say I am coming over tomorrow morning to hear about her potentially illegal news. She says to bring Sad Ed as she needs three of us for it to work. Oh God, hope it is not some three-way 'friends with benefits' sex orgy. Suzy is always trying to promote them.

Wednesday 22

It is not a three-way sex orgy. It is Wicca! Scarlet had a revelation at her Auntie Sadie's and has decided to form a coven, as it is the ultimate in pro-women, pseudo-goth activity. Me and Sad Ed are going to be in it too as three is some sort of mystical number. I did point out that Sad Ed is not strictly female, but Scarlet says she thinks hc has excess oestrogen (hence the bingo wings and manbreasts) and anyway, he can be our Spike. So I bagged to be Buffy but Scarlet says she is Buffy and I am Willow, which is not fair as I am utterly Buffy-like, but then we remembered that we are our own people and do not need to be fictional vampire-fighters so we agreed to drop the whole Buffy thing and stick with our real names (although Rachel is not at all Wicca. May change it to Hemlock or something). Scarlet's cats Gordon and Tony are going to be our familiars. I did offer the dog but she says dogs are utterly non-Wicca, plus he is bound to eat our sacred implements, when we get them. (This is true, although Gordon and Tony did not show any potential familiar activity, i.e. they spent all morning licking their genitals.) I said it was utterly brilliant as will be able to cast love spells and hook Justin into my Wicca web and possibly give Sophie warts or something. But Scarlet said we will be using our powers to do good in the world, not meddle in the affairs of ex-lovers. She is right. Although I bet she is plotting something for bat boy Trevor.

We are starting on Friday, once GCSE results are out of

the way. Apparently the worry will be sapping our Wicca Power at the moment so it is best to wait. Then we all started worrying about GCSEs and had to eat an entire packet of Waitrose chocolate florentines and watch classic *Deal or No Deal* to calm down.

. . . .

Thursday 23

8.30 a.m.

There is an air of general GCSE-related doom hanging over Summerdale Road. Mum is trying to pretend that she is not concerned. She actually said she will love me whatever my grades. This is not true. Her love is entirely correlated to academic prowess. This is why James is her favourite as he is naturally boffin-like. Then she offered to drive me to school in the Fiesta so that we can be first in the queue. I said not to bother as Mrs Leech (school secretary—bad hair, too much face powder, biscuit habit) is bound to have lost them under a packet of bourbons and we will be lucky to get any information before lunch-time. This is partially true. Although mostly I do not want Mum stalking round John Major playground like some Marks and Spencer-clad madwoman. I will never live it down. Me, Scarlet, and Sad Ed are going together. Bob is picking me up at ten in the smelly Volvo. I said it wasn't very witchlike, but Scarlet claims she is going to hang sacred herbs from the rear-view mirror to empower it. And cover up the lingering odour of sick.

9.45 a.m.

Oh God. This is it. Am utterly traumatized. My entire literary and generally brilliant future depends on whether or not I remembered the valency of boron etc. If only Hilary were here with his calming arm-squeezing ways.

9.55 a.m.

Sick smelling Volvo has arrived. In less than an hour will know my fate.

12 noon

Fate still unclear. GCSE results locked in school office and Mrs Leech has lost key. School caretaker Lou (former Criminal and Retard, once ate school rabbit) is looking for his spares. On plus side, Thin Kylie has brought several bottles of Strongbow in anticipation of being the first Britcher to get a qualification. Mum clearly has less faith in me than Cherie as she is ringing every five minutes to check progress. Have turned phone off as pressure may send me over edge. Will just have sip of cider to calm nerves. It is mostly apples anyway so is almost health-giving.

4 p.m.

Am bit drunk. It is because did not get results until three when Mark Lambert gave Mrs Leech a leggy into the office window (it is lucky she was wearing trousers or the view could have been potentially scarring) and in meantime have consumed half a litre of Strongbow. But do not care. As am utter genius. Have passed all GCSEs— two As, six Bs and only one C grade, i.e. maths, which is pointless subject anyway and will never need it again. Scarlet got five As and four Bs and Sad Ed got nine Bs. He said that is his destiny in life, to be second best. He is secretly happy though. I saw him smile when Thin Kylie fell off the sheep fence. She got three Ds and is ecstatic. Even Mark Lambert got one (French, unbelievably). Mrs Duddy says it is her best Retards and Criminals cohort ever i.e. twenty-seven GCSEs at E grade or above (among thirty-one pupils). Even Mr Wilmott seemed satisfied. Although, according to Mrs Leech (wild with abandon after eight gypsy creams and a Hooch) he was on the phone to Burger King Sports Academy all morning trying to wheedle their grade point average out of Mr Medwell.

5 p.m.
James says I may have frittered my life away by only securing a C in maths. He says I will regret my casual attitude when I am struggling to secure employment now that an economic downturn is on the horizon. He is an idiot. At least Mum is more philosophical. She says I can use my A Levels to make up for my disappointment. Although she is not so philosophical about me tripping over the dog and spilling an illicit carton of Ribena on the hall carpet. Am in room now with a packet of Jacob's Cream Crackers, a bottle of Volvic, and instructions to

sober up before *Neighbours*. May just close eyes though. It is all the overexcitement. Mum is wrong about disappointment. Today has been a milestone in my formative years and will look back on it with pride (except bit where mistook sheep poo for Malteser).

. . . .

Friday 24
9 a.m.
Have headache. Wish was witch already so could cast spell to despatch nausea and pain. Instead will have to drag self to bathroom for Anadin. Yesterday was colossal mistake. Am not genius. Am average. As usual. And am never drinking Strongbow again. It is stealth alcohol, i.e. makes you think it is lovely vitamin-filled appley stuff but is evil deathly poison. Plus am due at Scarlet's at eleven for our inaugural coven meeting. Hope do not have to do any actual witchery as think powers may have been depleted by cider.

5 p.m.
Did not have to do any casting of spells yet. Scarlet says we are only novices and must do some background reading first. And buy some essential witch gadgets, i.e. pentacles and wands. We are going to Cambridge next week, as Saffron Walden is understocked when it comes to occult accoutrements. Suzy is very excited by it all. She says paganism is the true religion and that we will

be at one with Mother Nature, Gaia, and various other feminine deities. Jack says we are fooling ourselves. He is against all things paranormal. It is his communist tendencies. Edna the non-Filipina Labour-friendly cleaner did not seem too happy either. Scarlet says it is only because she thinks she will be mopping bat blood off the Habitat rugs. I asked if that was at all likely. Scarlet said no. Although there might be some goat bits. I don't know why Edna is so touchy anyway, mostly she spends her time hoovering up the trail of Benson and Hedges ash that she leaves behind when she is dusting.

Saturday 25

Have had some excellent news at work. Am getting a pay rise, i.e. £2.85 an hour, a 15p cash terms increase! It is not much, but it is the principle. It is because me and Jack did some severe lobbying, i.e. I pointed out I had several GCSEs now, including chemistry and maths, so was more qualified to sell vitamins and add up lentil bills. Then Jack baffled him with a speech about trade union rights and spinning Jennys. It is excellent as debt mountain has notched up several inches due to Bruce killing Sad Ed's iPod plus Mum is making me pay Granny Clegg back £50 out of her emergency Nescafé jar. (I said *Vogue*, *Elle*, *Cosmo*, etc. were emergencies, given the lack of intellectual stimulation in St Slaughter, but she is not convinced.) I think Mr Goldstein was glad to have me back. Scarlet is clearly not cut out for menial labour. Apparently she got all faint after Mr Goldstein made her restock the notoriously high-up yeast extract shelf. It is her previous hardline goth tendencies. All the black clothes and staying in the dark have depleted her Vitamin D.

Also, apparently Saffron Walden has been a hotbed of employment-related shake-ups in my absence. Trainee butcher Justin has been replaced by Dean 'the dwarf' Denley. I know it is a good thing, i.e. because I am utterly not supposed to be mooning about after Justin. But Dean has weedy arms and crap hair. Plus he has to stand on a box to do any mincing. It is not at all inspiring.

Sunday 26

Was going to do witch revision today but Mum said we are all going to church as Baby Jesus is getting christened in anticipation of appointment of St Regina's go-getting Superhead. I said I couldn't go as *a*) am baptized into mental Cornish church and do not want to enrage Methodist God by crossing threshold of run-of-mill Church of England and *b*) Grandpa Riley only invited the dog due to the ridiculous names hoo-ha. But Mum said he has relented during my exile and James and I are godparents. So Baby Jesus will have a deluded Ninja and a witch as his spiritual guides.

3 p.m.
Baby Jesus Harvey Nichols Riley is now an official member of St Regina's Parish Church, as witnessed by Rachel and James Riley, godparents and general lifestyle advisers. It was not an entirely hoo-ha-free ceremony, i.e. Treena managed to blaspheme several times during the proceedings due to presence of 'knickers up the chuff' and the dog drank the holy water. Grandpa got it in on the pretence of it being a guide dog for the blind (he put on his Reactolite glasses and tripped a bit). Reverend Begley (still fit enough for vicar duties, but not for managing 270 unruly children) said it was unusual-looking for a guide dog but Grandpa pointed out that in America they have seeing eye monkeys who can make scrambled eggs and all sorts so I think Reverend Begley thought he was getting off lightly compared to a troop of gibbons in the vestry. He is mistaken. Gibbons would be a breeze compared to the dog.

5 p.m.
Mum has asked why I am not wearing my brace. Said I was wearing it at night instead. Think she believed me.

Monday 27
Bank Holiday
6 a.m.
Mum is booking me an emergency appointment with Mrs Wong for brace replacement. She swooped in a

surprise fact-checking dawn raid. She is like Special Branch. When I am actual witch I will be able to befuddle her with my mystical aura though. She will be powerless in my presence. Possibly. Am going back to sleep now. Is bank holiday so no point even getting dressed. Scarlet is researching potential celebrity sex guests for Suzy, Sad Ed is at his cousins' in Leighton Buzzard, and the only shops open are Mr Patel's sticky lino emporium and BJ Video.

Tuesday 28

Thank God Bank Holiday is over. It is complete waste of a day, when I could have been usefully doing Wicca-related things. If I knew the first thing about witchcraft, obviously. Am going to library later to investigate its 'supernatural' section. And possibly write to Gordon Brown to suggest a reduction in national holidays. Mum is in agreement. She says they just clog up the roads with freedom-crazed office workers.

3 p.m.

Oh God. Something terrible and potentially Simple-Life threatening has occurred. It is nothing to do with library (supernatural section only useful if you want the *Usborne Guide to Ghost Hunting*). It is Justin. He is back. I know this because I managed to walk into him outside Gayhomes while I was being distracted by a display of wallpaper. It was awful. (Justin, I mean. The display was the usual precarious and uninspiring tableau.) We just stared at each other for what seemed like eternity, but was probably only five seconds. Then he said, 'All right?' and went into Eaden Lilley's. He was not buying anything. It was an escape route. He hates me so much he cannot bear to be within same road as me. Plus the impact made him spill Coke Zero all down his favourite Nirvana T-shirt. He rubs Kurt Cobain's face when he needs inspiration. It is like Samson's hair. He is powerless without it. So now have soiled his musical genius, to top all my other faults. He will never want me again. Which I know I am not supposed to care about as am utter Shania Twain-style powerful woman. But the thing is, I do. It is the dirty blond hair. And the dirty T-shirt. Oh God. The Simple Life just got complicated all over again. Am totally back in Phase One.

On plus side, Mrs Wong cannot fit me in until October so am disfigurement free for over a month. Though it is wasted as Justin cannot even bear to look at me.

- -

Wednesday 29

This is typical. You get chucked because you have min-uscule breasts and your dad did not invent Microwave Muffins and then, once you are depressingly single, your bust finally decides to make an appearance. Mum pointed out that I was developing a cup overhang (common, and

84

on par with tattoos or fake tan in her book), and that I should go to Booths and get measured immediately (declined as do not want Mrs Dyer (unconvincing dye job, fat feet, smells of Yardley, propagator of Sad Ed suicide rumours) manhandling breasts, so measured self instead using method recommended in 2002 *Just Seventeen* annual (previous owner Thin Kylie)). Am now 34B i.e. entire size bigger. But do not care any more. My breasts are nothing but empty vessels now.

5 p.m.
Ugh. Just reread that bit about empty vessels. That sounds vile. Especially having had to sit through Cherie's drunken 'why I had breast implant' rant, i.e. 'they were like two shrivelled socks'. Mine are not at all sock-like. But no one is going to want to touch them anyway. Am going to bed to mope and listen to 'our song' some more.

. . . .

Thursday 30
9 a.m.
James has confiscated my Arctic Monkeys CD. He says the perpetual Northern shouting is interfering with his Ninja calm. Also, he says he has sent for Scarlet and Sad Ed to liberate me from my wallowing. I said, on the contrary, it was more meditating on my fate. But am secretly glad. Need friends to listen to my torment. The dog is useless at this. It got bored after five minutes and

wandered off to lick the stair carpet. (James dropped a Mini Milk there last week and did his own mess removal. He has failed. The stain has gone but the taste lingers. Mum would be ashamed.)

5 p.m.
Am utterly back on track and in Phase Two again. It is because Jack says Justin is not coming back to Sixth Form. Rock Foundation at Braintree has been reprieved at the last minute after they promised to teach people to actually read music as well as nod and strum along to Pink Floyd. So he is going to pursue his career as a rock god. Am glad. Hopefully the twenty-mile commute will tear him and Sophie Microwave Muffins apart and then I will laugh at him when he comes crawling back to me. Gosh. Sound almost goddess-like. It is because am now in possession of genuine crystal necklace plus *Everything You Need to Know About Wicca* manual by Celestine Norton (long grey hair, mystical necklace, slightly mad look in eye). Scarlet has a sacred pentacle bowl and Sad Ed has a broom. It is not for flying (disappointingly) but is for sweeping away astral build-up. We couldn't find a cauldron so Scarlet is going to borrow Suzy's Nigella soup pot and draw some runes on it. We are going to do some revision and meet in a week to test our powers. And our wands. Apparently we have to choose our own, according to our Wiccan characters. Will get something literary-based, obviously. Maybe a replica of Harry Potter's one with the phoenix feather in it.

86

Also have three new bras (Mum-approved Marks and Spencer with no lace, no push-up padding, no Playboy symbols and an ample backstrap i.e. totally boy-repelling but at least are 34B and not 32A as previously). Sad Ed said he will be getting measured up if his current man breast weight gain continues. It is the depression. It is causing him to binge on Caramac.

Friday 31
10 a.m.
James has begged to be allowed to join the coven. It is because he read chapter one of my Wicca book while he was on the toilet this morning (he is either very fast reader or freakishly slow pooer). He is very excited by the prospect of supreme divine power and has promised to renounce the way of the Ninjas. He is going to burn his leotard later in a ritual sacrifice. I said that *a*) I did not think that Scarlet would be too happy with him joining and *b*) Mum has hidden the firelighters after the dog became inflammable with creosote last year. He is undeterred and says he and Mad Harry will form their own rival coven. Keanu is going to be their familiar. He is goblin-like and potentially evil.

2 p.m.
Summerdale Road is positively alive with people seizing the day and doing groundbreaking things. Mum has

joined a book group. It is excellent and practically like a coven, i.e. it is women only (Mum asked Dad if he wanted to join but he said he would rather chew tinfoil). Although do not think Marjory, Mrs Thomas, Mrs Noakes, and Cherie have any mystical powers. Mum was against Cherie joining but she got wind of it over the deli counter at Waitrose and demanded entry. Mum says there is no arguing with her once she has decided she wants something. It is Terry I feel sorry for. He is utterly wife-beaten. Anyway, they are taking it in turns to choose the book. It is Mum first. They are doing *The Last Family in England* in a fortnight. It is about modern family breakdown and has a Labrador as the narrator. It sounds utterly far-fetched to me. If our dog were narrating a book it would revolve entirely around furniture consumption. Although it might be enlightening as to why he is so anti Jon Snow. Mum cannot put Channel 4 on any more for fear of sending it into a panic. At least I could understand the Natasha Kaplinsky thing. Her lips are huge and her hair doesn't move. Thank God she has gone to Channel 5, which is forbidden in our house.

Am slightly concerned at potential Wicca powers. Did as book instructed and tried to manifest my goddess energy by rubbing my hands together and visualizing lightning but just got friction burn. Although it is early days yet. Will probably be breathing fire by end of the week. Still not chosen a wand yet either and James says it is sacrilege to try to recreate the phoenix-feather one and he will be hexing me if I even try. Have checked with Scarlet and she says any straight object is fine. So have narrowed choice down to extra-long novelty Fitzwilliam Museum pencil, Mum's electric fly swat, and a cheerleader baton left over from my and Sad Ed's brief majorette phase in Year Five.

ELECTRIC
FLY SWAT

KALIB

RACHEL RILEY
IS UPDATING
HER PROFILE

september

Saturday 1

Nuts In May is in turmoil again. Sad Ed's mum Mrs Thomas has quit. She says the 9 to 5 is interfering with her many and varied Aled Jones commitments. Mr Goldstein is back to the drawing board. He has even asked Jack if he might consider leaving school for a future in wholefood outlet assisting. Jack said no, as he is still hellbent on being an anti-war Foreign Secretary. I do not blame him. Lentils are not a career for any self respecting literary type. Besides, the till is demonic.

On plus side, have procured essential Wiccan herbs cinnamon and sage at ten per cent staff discount. Did not tell Mr Goldstein what they were for. He is Jewish and witchcraft of any kind is bound to compromise his Kosher ways. Said Mum was making Delia's shepherd's pie.

7 p.m.

Sad Ed just came round. He is having Wicca trouble. It is Mrs Thomas. She has been using the astral build-up broom to unclog the drains. He is worried it may have its energies tainted. I said Scarlet will be able to cleanse it for him with an incantation. Which is possibly true. On plus side, he says he is glad his mum is out of a job. It is not the Aled Jones stuff, it is his diet. He said the stress (and availability of discount Tofu etc.) was having an effect on his tea menu and staples like sausages and mash were being replaced by quinoa bake. Asked him how trolley herding is going. He says it is marginally better as Gary Fletcher is at his nan's caravan in Hunstanton for two weeks so he has been promoted. Asked what his extra responsibility involved. He said he has to oil the brakes and check for discarded plastic bags. It is hardly mettle-building stuff.

. . . .

Sunday 2

Have put down my Wiccan devices and am devoting entire day to preparation for school. It is serious business, i.e. no longer a matter of digging old kilt and blazer out of back of wardrobe and buying an array of Biros. Instead need entire weekly wardrobe plan, customized Converse, and literaryish fountain pen. Want to look edgy and utterly vintage, but not so much that outdo superior Upper Sixth and am not welcome on the saggy sofa. It is a fine balance. Trinity Braithwaite went too far last year when she came to school in a tutu. No one spoke to her for weeks.

James does not have to worry about these matters. It is because he is not back to school until Thursday. He says it is swings and roundabouts as far as INSET days are concerned. Mum is not so happy-go-lucky. Not only has she got him under her feet for three more days, it delays the grand revealing of the new Superhead.

7 p.m.

Think am finally ready. Wardrobe planned with military precision (with aid of James, an A3 sheet of graph paper, five highlighter pens, and some Teletubbies stickers). Am going for big first day impression i.e. Fifties dead lady dress. Then will introduce more vintage wear throughout week. Am saving ironic Brownie T-shirt until Friday, traditional 'go mad' day. Have customized bargain Army Surplus bag with Kooks badges (de rigueur in Sixth Form last year) and am going to take Arctic Monkeys CD in order to instil self with instant radical edge. Will be excellent and cannot wait to absorb heady atmosphere of academic prowess and youthful exuberance.

Monday 3
8 a.m.
Wardrobe chart undergone slight rejig. Mum had fit about the gaping hole, dead lady Fifties dress and sent me back upstairs to change so am now wearing denim mini with stripy 'French chic' top, which was Tuesday's outfit, meaning have had to move one-armed hairy jumper forward an entire week from next Wednesday. James is feverishly restickering the chart to reflect the rethink. But am now ready for Sixth Form appropriate breakfast of black coffee. It is compulsory not to eat until you get to Mr Patel's at first break.

8.15 a.m.
Although do not want to faint in hothouse atmosphere. Will just have bowl of Shreddies. Will tell Scarlet it was croissant. French patisserie is allowed as it is utterly cosmopolitan.

8.30 a.m.
Why is Thin Kylie leaving the house so early? *Jeremy Kyle* hasn't even started yet. She cannot be going to school. There is no way Mr Wilmott would let her stay on for A Levels. She only got three GCSEs and one of them was in Food Science.

4 p.m.
Thin Kylie *was* going to school. As was almost the entire cohort of Criminals and Retards. It is because Mr Wilmott has implemented an emergency go-getting measure, i.e. an entire vocational programme including BTEC Hair and Beauty, Bricklaying for Beginners, and Essential Car Mechanics. Scarlet says it is an excellent Labour party policy to put manual labour on a par with academic study. She is wrong. There is no way tinkering with a Datsun is the same as A Level Drama. And Mr Wilmott is not doing it to be left-wing. He is doing it because Burger King Sports Academy have got a new plumbing wing and he is worried we are losing out in the forward-thinking school stakes. He will regret it later when Mark Lambert has terrorized the sheep for another two years and half the Sixth Form are pregnant or on probation.

Also Goth Corners Mark II and III are in chaos. It is Scarlet and Trevor's on-again off-again love life. None of the trainee goths know who to sit with any more. Scarlet has been forced to take drastic measures and has instigated a new Coven Table in between the maths geeks and the hardcore drama freaks. Some of the smaller goths are already eyeing us with jealousy. It is because we are real witches, as opposed to pretend vampires. Even Sophie Jacobs looked a bit nervous. It is because Scarlet threatened to hex her in the upper school toilets. She is powerless without Justin to protect her. I predict Scarlet will soon be Queen of A and B Corridors, and Miss Microwave Muffins will be exiled to substandard D Corridor (i.e. the 'gym', Rural Studies, and Criminals and Retards).

Common room was excellent. Even got to sit on saggy sofa for five minutes (me and Scarlet ran from double English) before Pippa Newbold sauntered in from double geography and ousted us. Am going to ditch Army Surplus bag though. It is utterly last season, according to Scarlet. Everyone is using Waitrose reusable carrier bags to lug textbooks around this term.

Tuesday 4

Had first Philosophy lesson today. It was utterly mind-expanding. We had to discuss whether right and wrong actually exist or are constructs of culture. Mum would be proud—I came down firmly on the 'of course they bloody do' side. Scarlet was more for the construct argument on the grounds that it is not wrong to murder a rapist.

Plus Mr Wilmott has agreed to swap French for Politics. As long as I get a letter off Mum. Hurrah.

5 p.m.
Mum has refused to let me swap French for Politics. She says there is no way she is letting me fritter my future away on a subject that is the province of self-promoters and notorious philanderers. She has offered Physics as a halfway measure. Have declined. The only people doing Physics are the mathletes. Plus it is taught by Mr Potter who smells worse than Oona.

7 p.m.
Am doing Politics after all. It is not because Mum has relented. It is because James has forged me a freakishly authentic letter. Not only is the handwriting almost identical, but the tone is both pedantic and menacing. By the time she finds out, I will be baffling her with my knowledge of Keynesian economics. And I can always watch *Chocolat* if I need to speak any French.

. . . .

Wednesday 5
8 a.m.
Summerdale Road is awash with St Regina's Superhead anticipation. James has had hair slicked down with industrial strength Brylcreem and Mum is wearing a skirt. Even the dog is strangely neat-looking, though there is no

way Mum would let him near school. The potential for devastation is enormous.

4 p.m.
The new Superhead is not so super after all. He is not from tough inner-city comp or fast-tracked from a high-flying job in the city. He is from round the corner, i.e. it is sandal-wearing Nigel Pendleton, next-door neighbour of Scarlet, and fellow left-wingish and vegetarian friend of Suzy and Bob. Worse, he has asked everyone, including pupils, to call him 'Nige' as it imbues a more age-appropriate casual, friendly air. Mum is not in agreement. She says St Regina's will be in special measures by half term if he persists with this lack of footwear and lackadaisical names strategy. She could be right. I do not fancy his chances in the face of Keanu and Maggot. James is happy though. He says he is going to tell Nige about his coven idea tomorrow. I reminded him that paganism does not usually go down well at Church of England establishments. But, according to James, Nige has encouraged everyone to expand their horizons, and he says his door and mind are always open to new ideas.

Thursday 6
James has abandoned his coven. Not because Nige shut his door, or his mind. It is more Mad Harry's mind. He says it is too girly. (But wearing a leotard and tights and

doing expressive dance is fuelled with testosterone?) Anyway, they have decided to become ghost hunters instead. James says they have unearthed an ancient and prophetic manual at the library.

6 p.m.
It is not ancient and prophetic manual. It is the *Usborne Guide to Ghost Hunting*. Have just seen James reading it in bath.

. . . .

Friday 7

School has gone Facebook mad. Which is quite progressive for Saffron Walden, i.e. only several years after the rest of the country instead of an entire decade (we are still waiting for Boyzone to go out of fashion from the first time around). Me, Scarlet, and Sad Ed are going to do our profiles at the weekend. Jack says it is a false sense of community and utterly sad. He is wrong. It is brilliant. Sad Ed says we should go with MySpace as it is more band-orientated. But Scarlet says Facebook has Zombie fights and 'name that sweet' quizzes so we are definitely going down that route.

5 p.m.
James is investigating green ectoplasm in the downstairs toilet. Have pointed out that it is far more likely to be dog-related vomit, but James is not convinced. He thinks we could be under siege from creatures of the night.

6 p.m.

Is not ectoplasm. Is dog vomit, induced by it eating two cartons of Covent Garden pea and ham soup. James is visibly disappointed and has persuaded Dad to let him into the attic to look for unexplained presences. He is a moron. The only unexplained presences up there are Mum's 1980s jumpsuits.

7 p.m.

James says there is definite paranormal activity in the attic. He has heard scratching and, at several points, a cold shiver ran down his spine. Mum has sent Dad up to check for mice and missing roof tiles.

. . . .

Saturday 8

There has been more devastating news at Nuts In May. Ailment-ridden Rosamund is coming back! It is not that I don't like her (although the nits and flaky hands are a bit off-putting), it is that she works Saturdays so it means either Jack or I are going to be sacked, and join the ranks of idle unemployed. I said it should be Jack as he was last in and therefore first out, plus I am up to eyeballs in debt. But Jack said it should be a meritocracy, which is ultra left-wing and means who is best for the job. So then we had to be uber-efficient all day, i.e. no stealing Carob muffins, no organic tampon throwing fights, and no moaning when our fingers get stuck in the till of death. Mr Goldstein has promised to reveal his decision next week. I have no chance. Jack is far better at the till. And knew what homeopathic remedy to prescribe Marjory for her oral thrush. I tried to give her merc. sol. but apparently that is for mouth ulcers and could have set her recovery back weeks.

On plus side, James has done my Facebook profile for me. He is more technologically advanced than me, plus he has already done ones for him and Mad Harry. They are using them to promote their ghost hunting business 'Ghost Hustlers'. Which sounds like a gay goth band. Have pointed out that they are contravening several rules pertaining to age limits and commercial use (both Facebook's and Mum's) but James says he has the brain of a thirty year old. Which is possibly true. Plus no one will ever employ them anyway.

Mine is excellent. Although photo is one Sad Ed took for Glastonbury application, i.e. I look like a man, but crucially is not in any way pornographic (Mum has set rigorous parental controls already after she saw Thin Kylie's profile which is an underwear shot and also features Mark Lambert's right buttock). Have listed interests as literature, world events, and vintage clothing. Thin Kylie lists hers as puppies, 50 Cent, and arse (no idea). Have only got three friends so far (James, Scarlet, and Sad Ed). But am waiting to hear back from Sad Ed's ex Tuesday. Anyway, am not going for quantity, it is quality that counts. Am going to be discerning and only friend kindred spirit types, or celebrities. Unlike Thin Kylie who has seven O'Gradys and all of the Year Nine football team. Although they probably are kindred spirits to her. Plus have joined a group. It is 'Jane Austen is my Homegirl'. Am also looking into 'Jane Austen gave me unrealistic expectations of love', 'I love Mr Darcy', and 'I am totally a character in a Jane Austen novel'.

. . . .

Sunday 9

Rachel Riley and **Dog Riley** are now friends.

The dog is more advanced than me. Apparently it has had a profile for a month now (as designed by James). It has sixty-two friends and is in three groups: 'Dogs are better than cats', 'Dogs in clothes', and 'Pies are spanking gorgeous'.

Am going over to Scarlet's after lunch to test my Wiccan powers. Have decided to go with fly swat as wand. It makes spooky buzzing noise when it touches anything and has definite electrical energy. Have been practising with it since eight this morning. In between checking Facebook, obviously. (Still no reply from Tuesday in America. It must be the time difference. Or maybe she is scared that Sad Ed will track her down through me and cyberstalk her. It is highly possible. He has that look about him.)

5 p.m.
Am back from Scarlet's. Wiccan invocations not entirely successful. It may have been to do with the wands, i.e. an electric fly swat (me), bit of Habitat decorative willow

103

(Scarlet), and a plastic light sabre with missing batteries (Sad Ed). We were supposed to be doing visualization, i.e. thinking so hard about something that it actually appears. I went for a rabbit (I have always wanted one but Mum banned them on the grounds that their lifespan is woefully short and they eat their own poo and babies), Sad Ed tried for a Snickers (as he was missing vital afternoon snack for practice), and Scarlet did Jack Straw. But all that happened is that Sad Ed got dizzy from all the concentration and low blood sugar and had to have emergency hummus. So we got a bit bored and went on Facebook instead. Scarlet already has 187 friends including Gordon Brown, someone out of *Skins*, and three David Milibands. She was not sure which one was the real one (there were twenty-seven) so she has gone for the most boring profiles. Sad Ed has two: me and Scarlet, so at least am beating him. He is in five groups though: 'Jews who like Quavers' (he is not Jewish but does like Quavers and there was no 'depressive former choir boys who like Quavers'); 'If this group reaches 100,000 I will name my son Batman'; 'Put raisins back in Double Deckers'; 'Morrissey's invisible hand touches me when I sleep'; and 'What is with Lilo Lil's trousers?'

I pointed out that Barry the Blade (local madman, big beard, currently going out with Lilo Lil Simpson of wee-smelling white flares fame) might take exception and formulate some kind of hitlist but he said Barry sleeps in an Austin Allegro and is unlikely, therefore, to have internet access.

7 p.m.

Have now got thirty-five friends including Jack (who has joined Facebook on the grounds he can funnel serious friends to his MySpace page, which he has only joined as it is useful bandwise. He is still resolved not to regard it as real in any sense), Suzy (who has had a profile for a year and is friends with porn stars), several O'Gradys, and smelly lesbian Head Girl Oona Rickets. Plus have joined 'Retro is *not* the same as vintage', and the 'Back Doors Appreciation Society' (i.e. Justin's band. And I do appreciate his music. Just not his wayward groping), and have installed Superpoke.

9 p.m.

Scarlet has walled me to tell me to stop thinking about the Butcher's Boy.

10 p.m.

Dean 'the dwarf' Denley has friended me. That is nice.

• •

Monday 10

Rachel Riley has thrown a sheep at Dog Riley.

Facebook mania has overtaken the Sixth Form. The common room computer (no Pentium inside, teastained, actually chugs when switched on) has mysteriously disappeared and the IT room has a queue stretching down past the B Corridor fire exit. The maths geeks, who all own their own MacBooks, and are wise to the potential money-making situation, are renting them out at £10 an hour in the upper school canteen.

5 p.m.
Have been poked by Dean 'the dwarf' Denley. Am messaging Scarlet immediately to find out the significance of this event.

6 p.m.
Oh God. It means he likes me. And not in a platonic Simple Life way but in a complicated erogenous way. It is Scarlet's ill-thought-out Butcher's Boy comment on wall. She did not make it clear enough which butcher's boy she meant. Have ignored poke. He will get hint and go away.

. . . .

Tuesday 11

Rachel Riley has been high-fiiived by Ed Thomas.

Scarlet has two new Facebook friends. They are Tamsin Watts and Tamsin Bacon (pseudo-identical twin Year Ten EMOs who obviously ring each other at 7 a.m. to co-ordinate hair accessories and stripy tights). But they are not limiting their friendship to cyberspace. They have taken to following Scarlet round corridors between lessons like Tim Burtonesque corpse bridesmaids. Scarlet says it is all part of being a Sixth Form icon, and a witch. Sad Ed agrees—Fat

Kylie followed him all the way from the toilet to Mr Patel's at break. Though it was possibly to scrounge his Nice 'n' Spicy Nik Naks. Did not mention that Dean the Dwarf had poked me twice during *Look East*. Am still ignoring him. He will go away eventually and find someone his own size.

. . . .

Wednesday 12

Dean Denley has caressed Rachel Riley.

Rachel Riley has karate chopped Dean Denley.

Ignoring not working. Instead am following James's method of engaging in Superpoke warfare. He is hoping it will catch on at St Regina's and he will be crowned first toughest in cyberspace, beating Keanu who is not allowed on the computers at school after he removed all the keys and rearranged them, thus turning 'DOG' into 'GAY' and 'CATS' into 'SHIT'.

Also Mum is beside herself with newly invigorated Superhead fervour. It is not not-so-super Nige. It is notoriously ineffectual Mr Wilmott. He has sent a letter home telling parents that John Major High is going to implement the Government's trailblazing Talented and Gifted Pupil Programme. He says it will counterbalance the special attention given to the Criminals and Retards (he did not say this, he said 'slow') by giving brainy people an extra boost. Mum is determined I am going to

107

be picked and has written to Mr Wilmott suggesting me. She is wasting her time. It will be the mathletes and teen mum Emily Reeve, who is still ahead of the pack, brain-wise, despite having no sleep and stitches in her hoo-ha.

7 p.m.

Although I am quite talented and gifted in the dramatic and literary areas, i.e. I know all of Ophelia's lines in *Hamlet* off by heart, plus have watched *Pride and Prejudice* thirty-four times. It could mean I get days off to visit Stratford-on-Avon and have one-to-one voice coaching lessons with Trevor Nunn. Hurrah.

. . . .

Thursday 13

Jewish New Year/Ramadan

Dean Denley has given chocolate to Rachel Riley.

Rachel Riley has thrown Tiramisu at Dean Denley.

9 a.m.

Have delivered letter personally to Mrs Leech, gatekeeper to Superhead Mr Wilmott, in anticipation of Trevor Nunn lessons.

10 a.m.

Am going to ask Mrs Leech to intercept Mum's letter and redirect it to the bin before Mr Wilmott sees it and bestows me with honours. Being talented and gifted does not mean one-to-one lessons with Trevor Nunn at the RSC. It means quizzes printed off BBC Bitesize in the mobile block with pervert-in-school Mr Vaughan.

11 a.m.

Mrs Leech cannot find letter due to non-existence of filing system and vast quantity of Peak Freans on desk. She says not to worry as there are only five places and they are bound to go to the 'Asians'. She means Ali Hassan and the maths geeks, and sadistic Mrs Wong's son Alan who was *a*) once on *Junior Mastermind* (specialist subject: the life-cycle of the medusa jellyfish) and *b*) rumoured to be earmarked for the higher echelons of the triads, a rumour possibly perpetuated by himself.

5 p.m.

It is Mum's inaugural Ladies' Book Group tonight. She has printed out a list of questions and a multiple-choice quiz (with the aid of James who is already compiling the Queen Elizabeth pub quiz on a weekly basis for Grandpa Riley). It is utterly exciting and totally like *The Jane Austen Book Club*, but without that one from *Devil Wears Prada* and with more Kathy Bates types.

9 p.m.

Mum is back from Book Club. It was not at all like the Jane Austen one in the film. Apparently Mrs Noakes objected to the book on moral grounds, Cherie had only got to page seven, and Marjory had read *White Fang* by mistake. Only Mrs Thomas had actually got to the end of the right novel. But on the plus side she loved it as she once had a Labrador too. It didn't talk though. And was called Aled, predictably. They are doing *Lace* by Shirley Conran next. It is Cherie's choice. Mrs Noakes will go mental. I know for a fact there is some vile activity with a goldfish in there (Thin Kylie read it aloud on the sheep field in Year Eight as part of her unofficial sex education programme).

Friday 14

Scarlet Stone has used the force with David Miliband.

Saffron Walden music scene is in mourning. Rock legends the Back Doors have disbanded. Sad Ed got the call last night. It is because Justin says he will be working with real musicians from now on and cannot afford to have his technique tainted by amateurs. At least the Jack Stone Five are still going. Albeit there are now only three of them. I did offer to replace Tuesday as lead vocalist but Jack says it is more ironic with three. He is going to drum and sing from now on. They are playing Jack's eighteenth party tomorrow night at the Bernard Evans Youth Centre. We (i.e. the coven) are all going. Scarlet says we can channel our energies to illuminate Jack in a pool of spiritual light (the lighting 'rig' in there is restricted to on or off). It is lucky there is a free bar, as will be penniless and jobless by this time tomorrow. There is no way Mr Goldstein is going to choose me over Jack.

Saturday 15

Scarlet Stone has drunk dialled Trevor Pledger.

Oh my God. Jack got a car for his birthday. It is a purple vintage Beetle with ironic furry dice and a door that is held on with gaffer tape. He picked me up in it on the way to work. I said it was excellent. Though I was surprised he had gone for a polluting type and he should have asked for a Nissan Micra like Hilary, which is more environmentally-friendly, i.e. left wing. But Jack got huffy and said that Beetles are the original left-wing cars of the common people and that if I didn't like it I could walk so said I loved it as he is the only person I know with a car, bar the Passat, Fiesta, and sick-smelling Volvo. Although we had to park over a mile away from work anyway due to ferocious parking restrictions and Nuts In May's lack of staff car park.

Jack said it was right that we should travel in style anyway as it is a solemn occasion, i.e. our last day working together. He is right, it is sad. Jack is fun to work with, plus he has no ailments. And his legs are supposed to be hairy. Then we wished each other good luck and said may the best man/woman win. We are finding out at closing time. Mr Goldstein is refusing to tell us before in case whoever loses gets minty and refuses to do till duty for the rest of the day.

6 p.m.

Oh my God. Am still in work. Mr Goldstein picked me after all. It is utterly amazing. But tragic for Jack, obviously, as now he will not be able to fund his gaz-guzzling but left-wing car. I said sorry to him, but Jack said it was the right decision and the best woman won. And he'll still get to do holidays and sick cover (which in case of Rosamund could be frequent). I hope it does not ruin the party later. It is very exciting as it is our first ever Sixth Form party. Am utterly not going to get drunk on Pernod and Black and snog an O'Grady.

12 midnight

Am utterly not drunk. Do not understand it at all as drunk seven bottles of something called Kaliber. Maybe it is because am sixteen and have built up liver stamina, like Fat Kylie who can do twelve Bacardis and still walk the line. Anyway, virtue is intact and have not snogged an O'Grady, or Dean Denley who hung around all evening laughing at jokes that I was unaware I was even making. Unlike Scarlet, who drank too much Carlsberg and flashed her black bra at Trevor. Luckily he was wearing dark glasses to protect his vampiric batlike eyes from the stage lights and did not see her.

Interestingly, drunk Scarlet blurted out that Jack didn't lose his job at all. Apparently he quit this morning in order to concentrate on his A Levels. Maybe Suzy is going to fund his petrol after all. But it is still odd though as Jack said it was important for future antiwar Foreign Secretaries to work as well as study in order to keep in touch with the real world. Anyway, I gave him a hug after his set with the band and said thanks. He said, 'What, for the music?' I said, 'Something like that.' Do not want him to know that I know that it is not that I am best employee after all.

. . . .

Sunday 16

Dean Denley has hugged Rachel Riley.

Rachel Riley has hadoukened Dean Denley.

The coven has expanded. Apparently drunk Scarlet decided to let the Tamsins join last night and they were installed in the den in their identical witch costumes when me and Sad Ed showed up. Sad Ed said that, as a pro-feminist coven, we should all decide together who joins. But Scarlet said that, as founder, she is head witch and gets two votes. Jack (not in coven, but watching *Popworld* in hanging seventies love-swing thing) pointed out that that was very un-Labour and it should be one member, one vote, but Scarlet turned the TV off and told him to take his unspiritual earth-bound body into the kitchen. Anyway, we have agreed to admit them, as five is still quite a magical number, according to Celestine Norton. But they are only our apprentices and we still hold higher status. Although Tamsin Bacon claims she has already managed to make the devil appear before her. She is lying. Or on drugs.

Anyway, it is all systems go as far as the coven is concerned. It is because the Autumn Equinox is next Friday, and it is a special Wicca festival, i.e. our powers will be especially potent. We are having a sacred ritual ceremony to celebrate. Sad Ed suggested the den, as *Friday 13th Part something or other* is on TV, but according to Scarlet, Wicca is all about nature and so it has to be outdoors. We are going to use their anti-nuclear war Peace Garden instead. Then Sad Ed asked if we were going down the ritual nudity route so we had a vote. Scarlet (pro) lost four votes to two. There is no way I am running around naked in the Stones' back garden with Gordon and Tony and potentially non-go-getting Headmaster Nige ogling my nether regions from the sliding patio doors.

. . . .

Monday 17

Rachel Riley is friends with Alan Fletcher.

The Riley household has been thrown into moral panic. It is because a form has arrived asking for confirmation that Mr Ernest Riley (i.e. Grandpa) still lives here. If we say yes, it means we get a £200 winter fuel payment. Mum, who is normally ultra law-abiding, says she is tempted to say yes as he spends half the day round here with Baby Jesus watching telly with the central heating on full. James says Mum's reaction is common and is known as fake pensioner syndrome. He says he is extremely disappointed in her and has taken custody of the letter to deliver it by hand to Treena later.

But more excitingly, am now friends with Karl Kennedy off *Neighbours*, real name Alan Fletcher. Admittedly he has 10,654 friends, but am hoping for an invitation to the set, none the less. Plus got lift to school in Jack's Beetle. Was slightly squashed, what with presence of Scarlet, Sad Ed, and smelly Oona. And gaffer-taped door fell off outside Mr Patel's. But was still utterly vintage and cool. Having motorized transport is instant kudos in Sixth Form. Unless it is Mr Whippy's ice cream and shag van.

. . . .

Tuesday 18

Dean Denley has married Rachel Riley.

Rachel Riley has divorced Dean Denley.

Mum has asked if I want to go to France at Easter as practice for my A Level. Remembered I have yet to confess to my politics switch, due to not actually knowing anything yet as have just been watching *Yes, Minister* videos. So said no on grounds of last year's Ninja frog-eating chicken fiasco.

James has also declined but not on death chicken grounds. It is business-related. He says he is booked up until next June with ghost hunting investigations. Apparently Saffron Walden is being stalked by no less than three werewolves. He is deluded. At least one of them is freakishly hairy librarian Mr Knox.

Am going to have to improve political abilities fast. Was hoping to be fluent in polling and filibustering by now but am still struggling to remember when the NHS was invented. Will ask to borrow Jack's *West Wing* boxed set. It is much more modern and basic principles are bound to be the same as ours.

. . . .

Wednesday 19

Rachel Riley has joined 'Bartlett fans on Facebook unite!'

James is jubilant. It is because 'Nige' has implemented a new system for choosing teams in games. Everyone just decides which colour tabard they like best. I pointed out that this meant he could end up with twenty-eight on one team and two on the other but James says that is a fair consequence of forward-thinking. It is because Nige says getting picked last for games can be potentially scarring for a child. He is right. I am covered in wounds from netball, hockey, and rounders. It is not so much that am crap at sport (although am crap at sport). It is more that Miss Beadle (overweight; bulgy eyes like Joey in

116

Friends or rabbits with myxomatosis) and Miss Vicar (stick-thin; no breasts; facial hair) went through a phase of letting the Kylies be captains which meant me and Scarlet got left out due to 'lezzer legs' and 'shit hair'.

Mum was not so sympathetic. She said it was the beginning of a slippery slope and the 'Brains Badge' (sheriff-style giant star for cleverest in class—worn by James on no less than 137 occasions) will be the next thing to go. James said that it has already been binned, along with milk monitors and 'keeper of the playtime bell'. Mum is writing to the council. I left them to their philosophical PE arguments to go and watch *West Wing* with the dog. It is excellent and am definitely going to be political as well as a literary genius after university (and after have lived in bohemian squat in Camden). I would be ideal as press secretary CJ. Am going to practise talking and walking fast at same time.

7 p.m.

Have bruise on forehead and several on elbows due to talking and walking incidents. It is not that am not cut out to be political type, it is due to excessive furniture and dog in way.

* *

Thursday 20

Rachel Riley is not talented or gifted.

It is utterly predictable. Mr Wilmott has named his chosen few. They are Emily Reeve, Ali and Amir Hassan,

Alan Wong, and someone in Year Seven who can do quadratic equations. I know it is a plus thing, i.e. will not have to sit in draughty mobiles after school with Mr Big Nipples Vaughan, but it would be nice to be officially talented and gifted. Although am possibly neither as head of politics Mr Slatter (beard, Fairisle jumper, history of failing miserably in council elections) highlighted when he pointed out that England does not have a House of Representatives. It is not my fault that we are still stuck in the nineteenth century, parliament-wise.

Am depressed. Will go on Facebook for a bit and do some Zombie fighting.

1 a.m.
Mr Wilmott is wrong. Am utterly talented and gifted as have just scored 100 per cent on Name That Thundercat! Facebook quiz. Plus have poked someone. It is equally talented and gifted Hilary. Hurrah. Hopefully he will poke me back and we can do cyber snogging.

1.15 a.m.
In a platonic way.

- -

Friday 21
Autumn Equinox (i.e. important Wicca calendar date)

Kylie Britcher has poked Mark Lambert.

9 a.m.
Hilary has not poked me back yet. Maybe he is too busy with his five A Levels. Or cleaning Granny Clegg's outside privy. Anyway, have other things to think about as have remembered that am taking part in (non-naked) Wiccan ritual in Scarlet's garden later and am supposed to have honed my witching skills to perfection. Will have to do it in double Philosophy this afternoon. Wicca is utterly mind-expanding. Plus we are doing the existence of God, which is bound to end in tears.

7 p.m.
Am fully prepared for Wiccan ritual and potential spirit apparitions of all varieties. James has begged to be a witness in case he can do immediate ghost hunting, but have declined in case Suzy decides to join in, as she will definitely go naked. In fact it is unusual to see her in clothes these days. Hurrah, it is totally going to be like that bit in *The Craft* where the earth opens up and divine beings seep out into middle earth i.e. Scarlet's anti-nuclear-weapon Peace Garden.

11 p.m.
Divine beings did not seep out into Scarlet's back garden. In fact Wiccan ritual disappointing on several levels. Firstly, the Tamsins spent at least an hour arguing with Sad Ed as to where magnetic North was. Then Scarlet tripped over her cloak and dispersed the cinnamon over Sad Ed's

119

Reeboks. Then we discovered that Gordon had pooed in the pentacle in an utterly unWiccanlike fashion. Luckily Suzy had made lavender anti-breast-cancer Nigella cupcakes so we ate those and watched *Friday the 13th Part 27* (possibly) in the den after all. Scarlet says we need to wait for Hallowe'en, as it is higher up the calendar in importance stakes, plus the pentacle will not be smelling of cat faeces. She has given it to me to look after. Will guard it with my life.

. . . .

Saturday 22

Scarlet Stone has worshipped Gordon Brown.

Ailment-ridden Rosamund is back at Nuts In May. It turns out that Guru Derek was 'realigning' quite a few other chakras as well as hers. She says she is done with men and is devoting the rest of her life (she is twenty-eight) to finding a cure for impetigo. I told her about our Wiccan coven and she is very excited. She says it is very in touch with nature and all things homeopathic. She is going to act as our external herbal adviser. Asked her what herbs would get rid of idiot Dean 'the dwarf' Denley, who spent most of morning waving sausages suggestively through the window. She said, on the contrary, his shortness could be a magical sign and I should be embracing him. She is wrong. He is not magic. He is just an oversexed midget.

120

Was going to do some Wicca when I got home but James has borrowed the pentacle to test it for ghosts. I have no idea what his methods are but they seem to involve Mum's microwave Geiger counter and plaque revealing dental tablets.

Sunday 23

Rachel Riley has thrown a goblin at **Dog Riley**.

The dog has eaten the pentacle. James is livid as he says it was definitely supernatural, according to his ghostometer (i.e. microwave leak detector). I am livid as now have to purchase new pentacle before Scarlet finds out. Unless dog manages to poo it out whole. Which do not think will be physically possible.

Also why has Hilary not poked back yet? Maybe it is because it is Sunday and thus a holy non-poking sort of a day. Yes that will be it.

Monday 24

Rachel Riley and **Hilary Aneurin Bevan Nuamah** are friends.

There is trouble afoot on the saggy sofa. It is because Sophie Microwave Muffins has demanded that the Sixth Form Criminals and Retards (aka BTECers) are banned from the common room and use one of the mobiles or

Rat Corner as their HQ instead (she did not say 'HQ' she said 'youth club'). She says it is nothing to do with their intelligence, it is simply a question of overcrowding. It is a question of intelligence. Fat Kylie tried to climb on the microwave to retrieve a flump that Mark Lambert had successfully stuck to an *American Pie* poster and the door no longer shuts. Anyway, it is not happening as Jack and Oona overruled it for being non-Marxist and possibly weightist. So that shut her up. Hah. Plus had more excellent news when I got home. Hilary has finally poked me back. It was not the religious thing after all. It is because he has been on a Biology field trip to Wales for five days to look at seaweed. Am jubilant as now have access to his profile and can see everything he is up to.

5 p.m.
Am less jubilant. According to Hilary's profile his status is 'in a relationship with Paloma Jones'. So checked out her profile and she utterly looks Penelope Cruz, i.e. who used to go out with Tom Cruise before he brain washed Joey off *Dawson's Creek*. Plus she has Martin Sheen as a friend i.e. the President of the United States (*West Wing* version), which beats Karl Kennedy hands down. It is utterly depressing. Am going to have to befriend someone equally serious. I wonder if Nelson Mandela is on Facebook.

Tuesday 25

Rachel Riley has chest bumped Hilary Nuamah.

Scarlet Stone has tripped Rachel Riley.

Scarlet says my interest in Hilary is threatening my Simple Life pact, not to mention my position in the coven. She says all the Superpoking will sap my Wiccan potency and has told me to limit it to platonic activity. Although she does agree he looks utterly gorgeous in his photograph and his socialist credentials are impeccable.

Also, the coven has added political campaigning to its many services and spells. It is because Emily Reeve is sad at being separated from Lola Lambert Reeve all day and might leave school unless emergency childcare measures are implemented immediately. Scarlet is starting a campaign for a Sixth Form crèche. She says it is totally sexist not to have one and is going to cast a spell on Mr Wilmott to make him see the light. Jack has suggested a petition as well in case her magic is not strong enough yet. Mark Lambert has already signed up. Plus he has had a surprisingly good suggestion of having a fully fledged nursery so that the Criminals and Retards can learn to be childminders. He says he would definitely transfer off Bricklaying if BTEC Nursery Nursing was on offer as it is too cold outdoors and the bricks keep falling on his feet.

Wednesday 26

Scarlet Stone's stripper name is Gordon Braithwaite.

The crèche petition now has 358 signatures. Admittedly some of them might be fake, e.g. Obi Wan Kenobi. But, still, it is an excellent achievement. Not everyone is pro though. Sophie Microwave Muffins has started an anti-crèche campaign. She says it will just encourage the BTECers to get pregnant and it is bad enough they get paid to be at school as it is. What does she mean? Anyway, Scarlet says Sophie has no hope as she cast her spell on Mr Wilmott during *Gavin and Stacey* last night using her Habitat wand. She says she can feel his resolve melting under her goddess-like energy.

. . . .

Thursday 27

James Riley has scored 100 per cent in *Name That TV Detective*.

Have found out what Sophie Microwave Muffins meant about the BTECers getting paid to be at school. Scarlet says it is the Education Maintenance Allowance. They get £30 a week to study instead of hang around Barry Island smoking. She says it is an excellent New Labour policy aimed at getting more poor people into university. Which is utterly not fair. The government should be paying me to be philosophizing political novelist type. There are not enough of us in the world. May well take it up with Mr Wilmott later as he is clearly in a forward-thinking mood. He has ruled out a crèche but amazingly has ruled in Mark Lambert's BTEC Nursery Nursing. He says it will put us strides ahead of Burger King Sports Academy, but will have to wait until next year as it will take a while to convert the old pig shed. Emily Reeve has had good news too though. Mr Wilmott is so terrified of her leaving and bringing down his grade point average, he has agreed that she can bring Lola Lambert in on Wednesday afternoons while the rest of us do electives (aka 'swimming', aka hanging out at the Mocha). Scarlet is jubilant. She says her Wicca potential has been proven. Jack has said nothing. But I can tell his feet are firmly in the 'power of petitions' camp. Have not told Mum. She is already despairing of the education system what with Nige's new regime at St Regina's. This could send her over the edge and decide to home school. Which would be potentially appalling.

. . . .

Friday 28

James is up to something. He and Harry have shut themselves in his bedroom in the dark with the Hoover and the ghostometer. God knows what they are doing but Mum will go mental when she finds out. The Hoover has only just recovered from the time Dad used it to clean the dog. The dog has only just recovered as well.

. . . .

Saturday 29

Scarlet Stone is all woman.

There has been a love showdown in Nuts In May. Guru Derek came in after our herbal tea break to beg ailment-ridden Rosamund to return to his retreat. He says his aura has gone green and his chi has been depleted since she left (though I suspect he is enjoying a nit-free period). He is not at all what I expected from a sex cult leader i.e. he was not beardy or wearing orange robes. He was balding and wearing an M&S V-neck. Anyway Rosamund told him to go back to Steeple Bumpstead. It is because she has been empowered by our feminist stance. Plus Mr Goldstein offered her an extra twenty-five per cent staff discount if she stayed.

I asked her if she wanted to come to tonight's coven meeting but she said she has possible ringworm and it might be contagious. Am quite glad as it is a first in the history of the coven. We are meeting in non-magical, but sibling- and parent-free Summerdale Road. James is having a sleepover at Mad Harry's and Mum and Dad are going to dinner with Mr Wainwright and Mrs Wainwright Mark II.

8.30 p.m.
Oh my God. James is not sleeping at Mad Harry's after

126

all. The phone rang in the middle of *Casualty* (decreed essential viewing as some goths were getting burned in a nightclub fire) and it was Mrs Mad Harry ringing to say 'night night'. They have done the textbook fake sleepover trick, but failed to plan for the over-protective parent situation. They are amateurs. Anyway told Mrs Mad Harry they were already asleep as did not want to worry her. Instead we are going to use our coven visualization techniques to locate them. Psychics do it all the time with missing children and paedophiles, according to Scarlet. Have borrowed some Sharwood's spices and am going to sprinkle them on our makeshift altar (aka the John Lewis nest of side tables).

9 p.m.
Oooh. Spooky. It works. Kind of. We were just doing visualizing when the phone rang again. This time it was Marjory P.I. ringing to ask why James, Mad Harry, and the dog were sitting on the grave of George H. Huggins in the grounds of St Regina's with a flask of Bovril, a microwave radiation tester, and Mum's Hoover. (Had not even noticed dog was missing, despite freakish lack of vomit, noise, or chewed furniture.) I tried to divert the issue and demanded to know what Marjory was doing in the graveyard, but she says she is using her digital spyware trying to catch so-called graffiti 'artists' in the act. Said James and Mad Harry were on a school project as do not want her alerting Mum and Dad. We are going

to collect them immediately before all supernatural activity gets banned.

10 p.m.
James and Mad Harry now safely back in their polar explorer sleeping bags and dog safely back on sofa watching *Sweet Home Alabama*. It turns out that they had been on an overnight ghost stakeout and were lying in wait ready to hoover up the spirits when they emerged from the graves. I said the Hoover was not battery-operated but they said they had plugged it in to the Sunday School kitchen. (Apparently Reverend Begley leaves the door open in case wandering tinkers need shelter and food for the night. Or idiotic ten year olds.)

11 p.m.
Coven meetings have been banned. Mum says I cannot be trusted. It is because the lounge smells of cinnamon and the nest of tables is over waxy. She says it is a shame I am not more like James. Oh the irony.

. . . .

Sunday 30

Ed Thomas is half man, half biscuit.

Mum is in a foul mood. It is because the Hoover is refusing to work. She says she is minded to add it to my debt. James stayed silent throughout the argument. He feels no guilt. He says he is quite content to watch an innocent man go to the gallows if it protects his business interests.

To add to my debt woes, it is Sad Ed's birthday tomorrow and I have no money to buy him a present. Have rung Scarlet for advice. She says to bring the fly swat over after *Popworld* and we can do a special Wiccan money spell. I said I thought Wicca was more about doing righteous deeds, not amassing wealth, but she says her Aunt Sadie is always doing it for the lottery numbers and has won £10 at least seven times.

5 p.m.
Hurrah. Have done excellent spell. We rubbed the fly swat with patchouli oil and called upon the forces of the earth to find me the money to buy Sad Ed a new iPod and pay off Suzy (Glastonbury ticket), Dad (phone bill), and Ms Hopwood-White (savaged fake baby). So by this time tomorrow I may well be a millionaire!

NICOTINE PATCH →

October

Monday 1

Kylie Britcher is, like, gasping.

The common room is in chaos. It is because the legal smoking age has been raised to eighteen and now half the Sixth Form is suffering severe nicotine withdrawal. They are all exceptionally minty and there have been three fights over custody of the CD player remote and it is only half past nine.

Also, the spell did not work. At least, no money had appeared by breakfast so gave Sad Ed my old recorder for his birthday. Said it was a special mystical Wiccan instrument. He did not mind, as he was too busy being excited about his present from his mum and dad. It is not Aled Jones-related but is driving lessons! I said what was the point, considering he is still planning on an untimely death. But he said, *au contraire,* he is now hoping to follow in Marc Bolan's footsteps and crash his car headfirst into a tree.

2 p.m.

Mr Wilmott has been called to a riot in Mrs Duddy's room aka Criminals and Retards. It is the smoking ban. I do not think Gordon Brown has thought through the consequences fully. Even Mr Patel is up in arms. His entire empire is founded on underage smoking. He says the repayments on his Touareg are in jeopardy with the loss of income.

Tuesday 2

Ed Thomas loves you, Flash, but we only have fourteen hours to save the earth.

The common room is awash with UCAS madness. You cannot see the saggy sofa for media studies prospectuses. The maths geeks are in charge of the *Guardian Guide to University* and are doling out information on male:female ratios, average beer prices, and distance in miles to nearest IKEA. What happened to choosing an establishment for its academic record? At least Jack is following tradition. He is applying to Cambridge to do Social and Political Science. I told him Hilary was going to do medicine there, as he is utterly brainy and may even run the Union. Jack said, 'Yeah? Well, he's not in yet, is he.' Why is he so narky? You would think he would be delighted to have a fellow left-wing applicant. Unless it is jealousy! Maybe he is actually still in love with me and my pro-Hilary/ anti-men stance is fanning his flames of passion. Excellent. Although obviously do not fancy Jack. Or any man for that matter. As am devoted to self-discovery (philosophical kind, not the sort Suzy promotes) and witchcraft.

Also, Mr Patel has discovered a new way to extract money from the hordes of cigarette-dependent children at John Major High. It is nicotine patches and gum on a buy-one-get-one-free deal. Thin Kylie has got five on one arm and is chewing as well.

4 p.m.

Our kitchen has been taken over by application madness as well. It is because James has to apply for secondary by the end of the month. He and Mum are going through SAT test results and value-added measures with a calculator and a pie chart system. I said I did not remember Mum being so rigorous when it came to choosing a school for me. Mum said my needs were not so complex. Plus I refused to go to Herts and Essex on grounds of brown uniform and Scarlet was boycotting Newport Grammar because Hugo Thorndyke (evil MP for Saffron Walden and environs) was on the board of governors.

- -

Wednesday 3

Kylie O'Grady believes she can fly, she believes she can touch the sky.

Mr Wilmott has banned nicotine patches from school. It is because five people collapsed in the common room from overdoses. Fat Kylie was wearing twenty-four at the time and had to be brought down with two of Miss Leech's emergency Valium.

Also, Scarlet is right. With every yin comes a yang. Hilary is definitely applying to Cambridge, which means he will be only thirteen miles up the A11 from next September. But it turns out that Paloma is already at Oxford 'reading' maths. So not only is she brainy and beautiful, it means she is an older woman i.e. utterly exotic. May cast spell on her.

4 p.m.
Unless she is one of those freakish people who go to university at the age of fifteen and have no social skills and end up with mental issues.

4.15 p.m.
No, have checked on Facebook. She is definitely nineteen. Curse her.

· ·

Thursday 4

Rachel Riley is away from her desk.

A terrible thing has happened. Mum watched *Watchdog* last night (her favourite paranoia-inducing programme) and is in a Facebook identity theft panic. She says evil criminals prey on idiots like me who post all their personal information on the interwebnet, and then they raid their bank accounts and steal their houses or else groom them for abuse. I said that as my Post Office account had a grand total of £1.04 in it, and my picture looks like someone out of Led Zeppelin, I hardly think they will be cyberstalking me, but she is unconvinced. She has banned all use of Facebook, MySpace, and Bebo pending further investigation. As if I would use Bebo. It is inferior in every way.

136

James is livid as well. He says it could seriously compromise Ghost Hustlers. He is going to use his special skills (i.e. Google, endless statistics, and air of cleverness) to persuade Mum to change her mind. I said I would try too but he said it is better if I stay clear of all discussions.

8 p.m.
God, there is nothing to do at home without Facebook. Have tried reading some philosophy but keep getting distracted by thoughts of who is Superpoking whom. It is worse than being grounded.

1 a.m.
Cannot sleep. What if Hilary has written on my wall and I miss it? Plus Scarlet's Zombies will have moved up another level and I will have no one left to bite. There is nothing else for it. Am going to have to pay Ali Hassan to use his MacBook at break tomorrow.

. . . .

Friday 5
8 a.m.
James and Mum have narrowed down their search for a secondary school. It is between John Major High, Newport Grammar, and St Gregory's Catholic Girls (now admitting boys and non-Catholics due to forward-thinking/desperate governors). Burger King Sports Academy has already been ruled out on the grounds that James's sporting

triumphs are limited to third place in last year's umbrella and yoghurt pot race. They are going to visit all three next week for their live final.

Asked James how his 'bring back Facebook' campaign was going. He said, 'Softly, softly, catchee monkey.' Have no idea what that means but he had better hurry up. Have had to use last of small change in my Postman Pat moneybox to fund my lunchtime computer session.

4 p.m.
Mum has banned use of Facebook on all computers, whether they are within her jurisdiction of 24 Summerdale Road or not. It is because she got James to do a spot check on my profile and saw that I had used the force with Hilary less than two hours ago.

. . . .

Saturday 6
8 a.m.
Have got to go to work. But am worried that absence of abusing Dean Denley on Superpoke may give him wrong impression that actually like him and he may cross King Street in his meaty apron and try to snog me. James says I am not to worry as it is D-Day in his campaign and he is going to work his magic on Mum while I am safely out of the house. I do not hold out much hope. Mum is not easily swayed. Not even by a force as persuasive and pedantic as James.

138

6 p.m.

Oh my God. James is miracle worker. Mum has agreed to reinstate Facebook, with the following caveats:

- no posting date of birth;
- no posting photographs of relations in bath naked, not even when they are two;
- no pretending to be the dog online, it is a menace in real life enough as it is;
- no friending people you don't actually know;
- no friending people you think you 'know' but who are actually fictional characters or potential rapists pretending to be David Miliband.

I asked James how he had done it but he said it is down to his secret powers of mind over matter. Anyway, do not care. Have already trodden on Dean Denley, had four Zombie fights, and raked my green patch. Hurrah! James is banned completely for being underage but he says Ghost Hustlers get enough business via word of mouth. Clearly there are way too many mad people in Saffron Walden.

· ·

Sunday 7

Dean Denley has served soup to Rachel Riley.

Rachel Riley has served Dean Denley as soup.

It was coven this afternoon but when me and Sad Ed

got there (admittedly via Mr Patel's for stocks of energy-giving, yet surprisingly low in calories, Maltesers) the Tamsins were already in the den with Scarlet trying to visualize their auras. Apparently they had been there all morning. Weirdly, they were dressed like her too i.e. channelling Helena Bonham Carter, i.e. black lace petticoat, stripy tights, and mental hair. I said to Scarlet it was a bit stalkerish and had they rung her up to check what she was wearing but she said no it is because they are natural witches and have immense psychic powers. She is fully expecting their periods to align soon. Sad Ed said what about his period. She said he can just have a giant mood swing instead of actual bleeding. Then she declared there was too much negative energy in the den for any spells so we made crisp sandwiches and watched *T4*. She is wrong about the Tamsins having natural powers though. Saw Jack in the kitchen when I went to get water to wash down claggy crisp bits and he said he saw one of them lurking behind the sick-smelling Volvo during *Popworld* trying to peer in the house for a glimpse of Scarlet.

When I got home James was testing Baby Jesus with his ghostometer in case he is the reincarnation of a historical king or scientific genius. There is no chance. Unless Einstein spent a large part of his formative years watching *Trisha* and eating Wotsits. The dog is in heaven though. It is because Jesus leaves an endless trail of orange crumbs in his wake and the dog is acting as a Hoover. Which is useful as the actual Hoover still hasn't recovered from its night as a ghost sucker in St Regina's graveyard. Mum is still baffled as to how ten crab apples and a shrew got inside the bag.

. . . .

Monday 8

Rachel Riley has added the Entourage application. She rolls fifty-three deep.

It is the first stage in Mum and James's secondary school elimination test. They are off to Newport Grammar this morning with a checklist, cunning questions, and a bacterial swab for the toilets. James is very excited as it is Jamie Oliver's old school and he is hoping to acquire some cooking genius skills through the corridor walls by power of osmosis. Mum is less excited as their SATs are several points below the expected level for a semi-rural South of England constituency with 75 per cent owner occupation.

4 p.m.
Newport Grammar has been ruled out on grounds of toilet hygiene. Also Mad Harry was there and Mrs Mad Harry says it is top of her list. Mum is hoping they will part ways next year and James will befriend someone more intellectually equal. And who doesn't encourage his idiotic Ninja/Ghost Hustling ways. I pointed out that Mum had said the same about Scarlet, but five years later

she is utterly brilliant and we are still best friends. Mum did not say anything.

Although am wondering about best friends bit. It is not Scarlet so much as the Tamsins. I know I should be embracing them in a sisterlike fashion as we are all one against men etc., etc. But they are hogging Scarlet at the Coven Table. Also, due to Mr Wilmott's 'no more than three abreast' in the corridors rule (following several crashing incidents in wake of *Mean Girls* phase), they are flanking Scarlet like limpet henchmen and I am forced to trail behind in coach class with Sad Ed.

Tuesday 9

Ed Thomas has opened a can of Whoop Ass.

The Tamsins are utterly getting on my nerves with their so-called psychic dressing and their hogging of Scarlet. I asked her if she wanted to come over after school to honour the Goddess Diana (the Wiccan one, not the real dead one) but Tamsin Bacon said she was too exhausted from double Economics. I said, 'What, too exhausted to even speak for herself?' And Tamsin Watts said they are not speaking for her—they are her. They are channelling her telepathically and can totally tell what she is thinking. Said, 'Is this true,' to Scarlet. Tamsin Bacon said yes. It is impossible to have a sane conversation while they are around so waited until they wafted off to GCSE science in

142

their identical ironic bunches. Then asked Scarlet if she wanted to come over. She said she was too exhausted from double Economics.

Sad Ed came over instead. Not to honour Diana. To mope. As usual. He agrees they are abusing their coven status as novices and that we should alert Scarlet to a possible takeover bid.

On plus side, I have a new friend on Facebook. It is someone called Robbie Lewis, who says he knows Jack through his band and recognized me from Velvet Elvis's first (and only) gig last term. Admittedly, I don't actually 'know' him (under Mum's strict criteria, this involves at least two years' acquaintance including several face-to-face meetings and preferably at least three friends in common), but he is eighteen and his photo looks like Johnny Borrell.

- -

Wednesday 10

Rachel Riley has used the force with Ed Thomas.

8 a.m.
It is day two of James's secondary school search. He and Mum have already set off on the arduous journey to Bishop's Stortford to assess the suitability of St Gregory's Catholic Girls. I fear it may fall at the first hurdle, i.e. the travel arrangements involve Len Viceroy and a bus full

143

of unsupervised adolescents. Am also leaving early to intercept Scarlet before Tamsins get to her and warn her of their evil plans for coven domination.

4 p.m.

Scarlet is totally unsympathetic to my theory on the Tamsins. She says their telepathic powers are just evidence that they are taking witchcraft seriously, unlike me and Sad Ed. I demanded proof but she said e.g. their wands are actual wands, not a fly swat and a light sabre. Talked to Sad Ed in free period (i.e. reading *Mojo* on the saggy sofa). He says we will just have to keep an eye on them for unsisterly activity. Scarlet is clearly blinded by their devotion and matching outfits. Their wands are not real, they are from Claire's Accessories. Mad Harry has one the same.

On different note, James and Mum are very excited by prospect of St Gregory's Girls. Apparently they have excellent IT facilities and the toilets are spotless. James says he is not put off by the journey, he will just wear headphones and listen to tapes of mathematical equations. Or Will Young. They are at John Major High tomorrow. I do not hold out hope for our less than adequate language 'labs', our mobile science room, and our questionable toilet facilities. Although we do have goats and multicoloured hoops in the gym cupboard. (The goats are not in the cupboard. They are on the field. Except that time Stacey O'Grady shut them in with the basketballs and Miss Vicar.)

Thursday 11

Robbie Lewis has high fiiived Rachel Riley.

It has been an utterly pants day.

1. AS Philosophy ended with a near riot during discussion on the equal distribution of money (Scarlet, me, and povvy people for, people from mock tudor mansions against).

2. The Tamsins are still speaking for Scarlet. Today Mrs Brain told Scarlet she had sold out of cheese baps and Tamsin Bacon said, in fake Scarlet voice, 'You shrivel-minded crone.' Tamsin got sent to Mr Wilmott. How long is she going to keep up this farce? Although it is true that Scarlet thinks Mrs Brain is a shrivel-minded crone. But then so does everyone.

3. Mum and James are putting John Major High at the bottom of their school list. Mum says the science labs are positively perilous. It is because the demonstration lesson was Mr Vaughan (pervert-in-school, supersized nipples, supposed French teacher but also Head of Drama and occasional chemistry due to woeful staff shortages) showing Seven Cheesmond how to make a baking soda volcano (elementary according to James). Apparently he got his chemicals mixed up and caused a minor explosion which broke the locust dome, and they escaped and caused a biblical style plague on C Corridor. Mum says it will be a wonder if

I pass my A Levels and that she will be signing me up for crammer in Cambridge next year if things do not improve.

8 p.m.
But have had yang to my crap day yin. Just got a message from Robbie Lewis on Facebook. He says he 'likes my style'. It is because I listed Young Knives and The Dead Kennedys as my favourite bands. They are not. Young Knives look like the Maths Club and have never even heard The Dead Kennedys, but Jack says they are seminal. Robbie says he is working on some music himself and would like to play it to me some time! It is amazing. I am an utter magnet to rock stars. First Jack, then Justin, and now Robbie. Although admittedly Justin dumped me. And Robbie may turn out to be mentalist with fake photo.

8.30 p.m.
No. He is definitely not mentalist. Have checked his friends and he knows Sad Ed, Fat Kylie, and James. Plus he lists *Pretty in Pink* as his favourite ever film. We are total soul mates. Even more than Hilary. Because even though he is not necessarily left-wing, he is single.

8.45 p.m.
Although he is possibly gay.

Friday 12

Ed Thomas has added the Petrolhead application.

Sad Ed has got his first driving lesson today. It is with Mike 'Wandering Hands' Majors (41, highlights, general causer of marital break-up, object of Dad's hatred) in one of his Ford Fiestas. Sad Ed is worried Mike might take a shine to him. He is deluded. Even if Mike was gay, there is no way he would go for Ed. He is not neat or nice-smelling enough. Gay men (unlike lesbian Oona) always smell nice. It is like a rule. Ed asked Mum if he could practise on our Fiesta in the driveway to acclimatize to its layout. He says he won't actually go anywhere, just fiddle with the knobs and levers. Mum has said no. She does not trust him not to accidentally snap the gear stick with his fat fingers. Sad Ed did not mind. He says he has natural driving talent and he will be steaming down the M11 at seventy within a week. He is deluded. Mike will make him do circles round Shire Hill for at least a month.

5 p.m.
It was worse than I thought. Mike did not even let Ed leave Loompits Avenue. He is operating a stationary lesson policy until pupils can prove they have mastered their right from their left and know which pedal is go and which is stop.

Saturday 13

Rachel Riley has challenged Jack Stone to a game of Scrabulous.

Work was unusually fraught today. It is because Thin Kylie came in with Mark Lambert to try to buy drugs i.e. Guarana gum. I think Mr Goldstein's hump and Rosamund's flaky eczema sent Thin Kylie over the edge because she refused to be served on the till by anyone except me in case she caught 'leprosy or mentalism'. So ended up with fingers trapped in till again for meagre 97 pence and burst into tears. Mr Goldstein has finally relented and is going to get someone to look at it. The till. Not my finger. That is wrapped in additive- (and glue-) free plaster.

Sunday 14

Jack Stone has beaten Rachel Riley at Scrabulous by 278 to 57.

Coven is off today. It is because Scarlet is going to see her mentor—Aunt Sadie. It is in preparation for Hallowe'en in a fortnight. Scarlet does not want a repeat of the Autumn Equinox pentacle poo fiasco. Which reminds me, need to get a pentacle as dog ate last one. Not sure if it is in or out as have not seen it since. But would not want to use it anyway. Mum is less squeamish. She just disinfects things once they have made their passage through the intestines. She says she is just being economical. She is being weird.

Anyway, am going to spend day doing useful and self-improving things instead, i.e. reading *White Teeth*, i.e. Zadie Smith's seminal novel about living in multicultural and gritty London. Will be like fantasy fiction for A Level students in Saffron Walden. The only grit we have is Barry the Blade and his ongoing habit of fishing in the bins for kebab bits. Will just check Facebook though in case have message from Robbie.

11 a.m.
Nothing as yet. Although my Zombie lieutenant has eaten several of Dean Denley's foot soldiers. Will start reading once have had brain-stimulating elevenses (rich teas and lemon barley. Mum is cutting back on Duchy Originals chocolate gingers. She says we are getting too much of a taste for the high life.)

3 p.m.
Got distracted by James and Mad Harry ghostbusting in the garage. They are convinced there is ghost residue behind the creosote. Still no message from Robbie. Will just do a bit more Zombie fighting.

4 p.m.
And maybe clean out my virtual aquarium.

5.30 p.m.
And eat dinner.

6.30 p.m.
Oh my God. It has happened. I got a message from Robbie during what would normally have been *Eggheads* but is now designated computer time (James and I have stopped watching this due to probability of Challengers winning dropping to 14,000 to one, according to James's calculations). He wants to meet me after school tomorrow down the Battleditches (aka Dogshit Alley, aka snoggers' paradise!). Have said yes. Mum would go bonkers if she knew, but am going to make Sad Ed come with me as protection. I would ask Scarlet but in current mode, i.e. ventriloquist act with the Tamsins, she might put him off. Oh hurrah. Am going to meet Razorlightesque soul mate at last and bond over seminal films and music. Will just phone Jack and get him to play Dead Kennedys down the phone to me so do not sound like complete idiot.

. . . .

Monday 15

Rachel Riley is away from her desk again.

8 a.m.
Have texted Sad Ed to check he is still on for tonight. He has agreed, but is not entirely happy with proceedings due to it possibly breaching Simple Life pact etc., etc., but have pointed out that it is entirely non-sexual (at the moment) and anyway I saw him ogling Tamsin Bacon's

150

black lace goth bra last week and I did not tell Scarlet so he owes me.

5 p.m.

Meeting did not go entirely as planned. Mainly because I have been the victim of a cunning online identity theft honeytrap thingy, i.e. it was not an actual real meeting. It was an evil trap, laid by Mum and her demonic assistant James. It turns out Robbie Lewis is not a real person at all. He is James, in one of his many internet guises, using a name stolen from a detective TV series and a picture of Johnny Borrell pasted from the MTV website. Mum made him lure me into his clutches to prove that I am incapable of using Facebook responsibly. It was utterly humiliating. James walked up with the dog and said, 'Waiting for anyone?' I said no, we were trying to commune with dead Saxons in a witchlike manner. James said, 'Oh really. And I suppose the name Robbie Lewis means nothing to you, then.' Then Mum leapt out from behind a conker tree and immediately imposed an internet ban. She says James could easily have been a paedophile or a murderer and I am lucky that it is her hiding in the bushes. She is wrong. A murderer would be easier to outwit. Sad Ed caved under pressure immediately. He told Mum he had begged me not to go and was only there to protect my innocence. He has no stamina.

Begged Mum to change her mind but she says until I can prove I am a responsible adult, there is to be no social

151

networking of any kind. James is utter stooge. Am going to plot his downfall immediately, as have nothing to do now that Facebook is out of bounds. Will pretend to be a vampire and lure him to possible drowning on the slide of death.

5.30 p.m.
Mum has just told me not to even think of plotting revenge against James or she will come down on me like a tonne of bricks. She is like Mel Gibson in that crap film where he can tell what women are thinking all the time. Except without the bouffant hair and alcohol issues.

. . . .

Tuesday 16
8 a.m.
What is the point of doing anything if you can't tell your 126 closest Facebook friends what you are up to? Am itching to Superpoke somebody. Even Dean Denley. But Mum is watching the computer like a hawk. Plus she has got James to block my Facebook account and set up several complicated passwords and a firewall. Not even Dad can get through them to check the golf results. He has gone round to Clive's instead, who has no security. And Nutella.

4 p.m.
It is worse than I thought. Not having access to Facebook is moving me rapidly down the coven hierarchy. Scarlet

and the Tamsins were Superpoking until midnight last night. Plus the entire common room has formed a new group. It is 'Who tipped Nutriment on the saggy sofa?' Begged Sad Ed to try to work out what James has changed my password to (it is not Shredder, Aragorn, or Einstein—checked on Ali Hassan's MacBook at a cost of £2.45 in first break (he has started a credit book for me due to hopeless state of finances)) but Ed says it is more than his life is worth. This is possibly true. James is unmovable as well. He says I am lucky to be alive and should be thanking him, not moaning and trying to get the dog to eat his ghostometer.

Wednesday 17

Still no Facebook access. Mum says I have yet to convince her I am not going to do anything stupid. (This is because I let the dog in the shower this morning and it ate the soap and started foaming at the mouth and James thought it had rabies and called 999.) Thank God it is half term next week and I will not have to suffer the endless in-jokes or cheering from the saggy sofa when anyone friends a celebrity. Fat Kylie has got the one with bad skin out of Take That and Kerry Katona now. And Sophie Nipples Pervert has got half of *Hollyoaks*. I am an utter outcast. It is like at primary when everyone was playing *Grange Hill* and I had to do hopscotch on my own. Tried to do some Wicca and channel positive energy with my wand and my goddess altar (one of James's old Barbies and a Denby plate) but all the hoo-ha has sapped my skills. Am going to be ejected from coven if this carries on. Although at least am marginally more magical than Sad Ed. He broke his wand fighting Gary Fletcher in the Waitrose car park after work. They were trying to re-enact Anakin Skywalker versus Obi Wan Kenobi in *Revenge of the Sith*. It is sellotaped up now. Scarlet will go mental.

. . . .

Thursday 18

Cannot even speak to Mum to beg her for mercy this morning. She is locked in the bathroom with Shirley Conran's *Lace*. It is because it is book group tonight and she wants it fresh in her memory so she can out-opinion everybody. She is going to regret it. She will want to be cleansing her memory immediately if the bits Thin Kylie read out are anything to go by. James is in agreement. He says he read several chapters while he was waiting for a poltergeist to make an appearance in the dining room last night and it is shocking stuff. Although he says at least it has neo-feminist overtones and some excellent equestrianism. Have no idea what he is talking about. But it sounds sisterhoody. Maybe Mum and everyone will swap sexual secrets and release the bonds of conformity.

9 p.m.

There was no sexual secret swapping. And no releasing

of bonds. Instead there was an almighty argument about porn (Cherie—for, everyone else—against, Marjory—does fancying Trevor McDonald count?) and Mrs Noakes has formed a puritanical splinter book group, which is only going to do Catherine Cookson. Cherie is not invited. Mum is not joining either. She says there is only so much Northern suffering she can take. She is going to stick to arguing about Jeffrey Archer with Dad. He has no strong opinions and bows to her greater knowledge at all times.

I noticed James 'borrowed' *Lace* while she was busy inspecting some dog-related damage on the sideboard. Will note information in brain for potential revenge.

Friday 19
Hurrah, it is half term. James is jubilant. It is because environment-mad Nige has set Year Six a holiday project. They have to work out the size of their family's carbon footprint and find ways to reduce it. James is taking it very seriously. He is hoping to harness paranormal energy, or the dog, and power the toaster with it.

Saturday 20
James has already started his environmental carbon footprint crackdown. He has imposed a strict 'no hot breakfast' rule, including toast. So had to have Marmite

on bread. Even the kettle is out of bounds so there is no tea. Dad told Mum to tell James to stop beggaring about, but Mum is backing him all the way. Not so much on green grounds but more because she does not want to be named and shamed in show and tell assembly. It is outrageous. How am I supposed to prepare for eight gruelling hours at the coalface, or lentilface, when have only had cold bread for breakfast?

. . . .

Sunday 21
8 a.m.
The carbon footprint thing is having an utterly detrimental effect on family relations chez Riley. It is only 8 a.m. and Mum has already shouted at Dad for leaving the telly and DVD player on standby after *Match of the Day* last night. He said he was sick of having to reset the clock every morning and, anyway, claims on standby consumption have been completely exaggerated. James has now shut himself in the meter cupboard with a torch to test the theory.

11 a.m.
Tests inconclusive. It appears leaving telly on standby may actually use up more energy than watching it. So Mum is thinking of banning TV altogether. But Dad pointed out that the results could have been skewed by Grandpa showing up halfway through and letting Baby Jesus blow-dry the dog. James says it is not that, it is the poltergeist

causing paranormal magnetism and making the dial whizz round. Have left them to their idiotic discussions. At least I still have a CD player in room and can listen to inspiring girl music, i.e. the Kates (Nash and Bush, the latter borrowed from Suzy who claims Kate based her 'hot hippy' look entirely on her) until it is time for coven.

11.15 a.m.
This carbon footprint thing is getting out of hand. James has now turned the electricity off completely. He says we should try to get by for at least a day without it. I said what about lunch? He said we can eat salad and nuts like our ancestors. He is mistaken. If the Cleggs are anything to go by our ancestors ate Fray Bentos and Viennetta.

12 midday
Electricity back on. It is because Baby Jesus goes berserk if he doesn't get to watch preschool kitchen menaces *Big Cook Little Cook*. Mum says no carbon footprint is worth putting up with that racket. Plus the freezer was starting to defrost and she had only just stocked up on organic pork loin.

7 p.m.
Am back from coven. Which was less than satisfying. Me and Sad Ed had to watch while Scarlet and the Tamsins performed their Hallowe'en salutation, complete with matching headwear. Tamsin Bacon actually said, 'Look and learn, amateurs.' It is outrageous. Wicca is not a

spectator sport. It is a divine expression of the power of nature and sisterhood, according to Celestine Norton. Sad Ed did not mind though. He just ate chocolate digestives in the loveswing. He says all the standing up and gesticulating plays havoc with his back.

To make matters worse, got home to find entire house in darkness. James has imposed a candles only rule. It is like being in a medieval castle (but with carpets and HobNobs). Though suppose atmosphere of gloom is quite literary and inspiring. Maybe will have genius novel idea and make fortune and buy coven and refuse to let Tamsins take part.

8 p.m.
Lights back on. The dog caught fire on one of the candles and tipped over the dining table in its frenzy to put out the flames.

. . . .

Monday 22
Half term

10 a.m.
There has been a horrific carbon footprint related incident. Am in shock and will have to lie down for a bit.

11 a.m.
Am slightly recovered now. Though still marginally

nauseous. It is because in his zeal for saving electricity James burst into the bathroom fully naked and climbed into my bath. He says sharing bath water is quite normal and that I have nothing to hide. He is wrong. It is not normal, except possibly in the Stones' house where wandering around naked is almost obligatory. Plus I have everything to hide. It was gross. Had to shriek for Mum to remove him immediately. But dog got excited by racket and tried to join in and now Mum is in mood because floor is soggy and is blaming me for overreacting. Am going round Scarlet's now for emergency counselling. Plus they are fully electricitied up and will be able to use appliances without fear of retribution.

2 p.m.
Scarlet was not in. According to Jack she is trying to summon the Goddess of the Waxing Light round at Tamsin's. I said which one. He said, 'Does it matter?' This is true. They are equally annoying. He let me in anyway to enjoy some energy wasting TV and use Suzy's diffuser as hair is in severe danger of looking like Fi Cunningham's Labradoodle if it does not get severe product and implement attention.

. . . .

Tuesday 23
Mum is tiring of the carbon footprint economy drive. James had her using sticky labels to remove crumbs from

the carpet this morning now that the Hoover is out of bounds. Although I noticed he was happy to use it yesterday when he thought there was an apparition in the toilet. There was not. It was Mum's Glade Wisp room deodorizer on overdrive. Also the dog keeps crashing into things in the darkness.

Still no sign of Scarlet. I rang earlier and Suzy said she was out with the Tamsins buying sacred purple cord at Booths but had left Hallowe'en homework instructions for me and Sad Ed. We have to practise weaving corn to make ritual fertility symbols. Will do it extra specially well, and also purchase superpowered pentacle so can win Scarlet back.

5 p.m.
Could not find corn so have woven moist wholemeal spaghetti. It is made of wheat so is utterly crop-based.

. . . .

Wednesday 24
Yet again my plans have been thwarted by James's ridiculous homework. Mum is refusing to drive me to occult-friendly Cambridge for emergency pentacle purchasing as it will clog the atmosphere with carbon emissions. She says there is nothing wrong with the shops in Saffron Walden and I will just have to improvise. She is lying. There is everything wrong with the shops in Saffron Walden. Am going into town though. Beggars

can't be choosers. As James points out on an almost daily basis.

4 p.m.
Am back from town and have witnessed something entirely suspicious. I saw one of the Tamsins (not sure which, but possibly Bacon as her hair is marginally higher) drinking Fanta with head goth and Scarlet's ex Trevor Pledger in the Mocha, despite him being declared an official enemy of the coven and therefore utterly out of bounds. She is plotting something. I can tell. Or maybe Scarlet is getting her to be a messenger and is actually planning to throw herself at his batlike mercy. If I had Facebook I could check for signs of illicit wall activity. It is entirely compromising, gossip-wise. On plus side, have bought pentacle. It is sort of circular china dish with interesting markings on it. Found it in Oxfam. It is bound to be some sort of Wicca relic.

. . . .

Thursday 25
Pentacle is not Wicca relic. Is James's ashtray (aka olive dish) from pottery last year. Mum had a clearout in the attic when James was doing his ghost hunting up there. Interesting markings are old Smartie lid imprints. I said she should be ashamed of herself, giving away the artworks of her precious children. What if one of us turns out to be Damian Hirst? She said if she kept all the tat we

161

brought home from school we would be knee deep in macramé owls and fingerpainted loo rolls by now. Plus there is no way James is going to be a painter. He does not like getting mess on his fingers. This is true. Anyway, will not let on provenance of pentacle to Scarlet. Will say it is genuine ancient artefact.

Friday 26

Something terrible and O'Grady related has happened. It is overwaxed eyebrows, i.e. mine. Fat Kylie did it round at Thin Kylies. They came over this morning begging for me to be a 'model' for beauty practice. They said they needed a total 'before case' so they could do one of those *Swan* makeovers. For some reason, possibly boredom due to internet and electricity ban, I said yes. So had to endure several minutes of pain and now have insane surprised expression. Plus I let them give me semi-permanent false eyelashes so resemble crap transvestite. Mum is livid. I pointed out that if we had Facebook I would be too busy to do idiotic things like this. She is weakening, I can tell.

Saturday 27

New transvestite look did not go down well at work. Mr Goldstein made me stay in the stockroom in case I put the hippies off their tofu. Rosamund says I am messing with my natural femininity. But she uses crystal deodorant and doesn't shave her legs so she is hardly a trustworthy source of beauty tips. Dean Denley did not seem put off. He offered me a battered sausage roll at lunchbreak. This was not a euphemism. Thank God. Declined though. Damaged meat products are just not as enticing from a midget.

On plus side, James's carbon footprint economy drive ends at seven tonight. James has begged to have it made permanent but Dad says it is cunning twist night in *Casualty* and he does not want to miss it. Plus Grandpa and Treena are coming over for Sunday lunch and they will not eat salad, not even in an emergency.

7.30 p.m.
Thank God. Have gone appliance mad and dried hair, epilated legs, whisked smoothies, and toasted four slices of granary. Dad has put the central heating on full and the TV, DVD, CD player, and SatNav on standby. James says we will regret it when we are all knee deep in polar ice cap meltwater, but Dad says he does not pay tax to live in third world conditions.

Sunday 28
End of British Summertime (i.e. clocks go back)
11 a.m.
There has been a royal scandal, according to Grandpa and Treena, purveyors of crap Sunday tabloids into the broadsheet environs of Summerdale Road. An unnamed

HRH has been caught on camera in a drugs and sex scandal. James says it is bound to be Harry as he is ginger and common. This secured him his second warning of the day. (He earned his first for trying to suck a shapeshifter out of the tumble dryer.) I do not rate his chances much. Mad Harry (not ginger, but common) is coming over later and they are bound to do something mental and dangerous.

5 p.m.
It is three strikes and out as far as James is concerned. He has been caught with his pants down. (Not literally, that would have been potentially horrendous—am still recovering from bath sharing trauma.) Mum found him and Mad Harry reading *Lace* in the shed. They had claimed they were whittling anti-vampire stakes. Mum is livid and has banned sex books permanently and any ghost-related activity for a week. James says she will regret it when Saffron Walden is overrun with creatures of the night. She says she will take her chances. Also Dad is in trouble. He pointed out that it was her book and therefore partially her fault. He is now weeding the runner bean patch.

I on other hand have played blinding hand by backing Mum all the way and an utter miracle has happened. She has relented over the Facebook ban (I pointed out that I had endured thirteen days of abstinence, whereas James only gets seven). Am now back online in the virtual arms of my cyberfriends. Hurrah. Have missed it so much. Pippa Newbold has been poking Stan Barret (once saw Paul

Weller in John Lewis), which is interesting, as two weeks ago she was poking Duncan Evans (resident common room 'DJ', i.e. has portable CD player and Pete Tong T-shirt). Also, more worryingly, Trevor Pledger is now friends with Tamsin Bacon. Have checked for poke activity, however there is no clear evidence on this. But interestingly this happened at 2 p.m. this afternoon, after she had phoned in sick to coven with depleted chi (coven subsequently cancelled as Tamsin Watts won't come without Tamsin Bacon, and Sad Ed was still in his pyjamas eating Minstrels and watching *Vanity Fair*). But am not dwelling on this because most importantly Hilary Nuamah has changed his status from 'in a relationship' to 'it's complicated'. What can this mean? Am going to message him immediately. Once have checked Paloma's status.

6 p.m.
Hurrah! Spanish beauty Paloma is 'complicated' too. So now coast is possibly clear for me to battle my urges and potentially resist Hilary's charms. Or not. Hurrah!

- -

Monday 29

Rachel Riley is saving the cheerleader to save the world.

Something is definitely afoot in Goth Corner Mark II. Trevor spent the entire lunch break staring at the Coven Table from over the top of his congealed blood (aka

Bonne Maman cherry jam) sandwiches. I pointed this out to Scarlet but she says he is obviously just still hung up on her, and that it is all quite pathetic. I hope she is right. Although I wish he would stop as his new contact lenses (all black) are entirely off-putting.

Cheered up when got home though. Hilary has confirmed my suspicions. He broke up with Paloma this morning. It is because she thinks she is in love with her long division tutor, Dr (not a real one, a made-up one) Whitaker. So clearly perverts are not limited to secondary schools but are happily embedded in universities as well. Anyway, Hilary says he is holding up OK but that it's good to 'see a friendly face', i.e. me. Have said he can use my virtual shoulder to cry on anytime. Oooh. Or maybe he will want real one and will hitch through the night to Saffron Walden and throw himself at my mercy as I am the only person to understand his alienation and sorrow.

Tuesday 30

Rachel Riley is Claire Bennet—angsty, paranoid, but kind of hot.

Ed Thomas is Hiro Nakamura—short, overweight, but with a sacred sword.

Hilary is still in Cornwall. According to Granny Clegg he dropped off two steak and kidney pies and a Sara Lee cheesecake (out of quarantine now that Grandpa Clegg has been assured it does not contain actual cheddar) on his way to school this morning. I said I was surprised the council were still paying for his services, considering her hip of doom was completely recovered, but she says Grandpa Clegg is enjoying having a 'servant' and takes to his bed every time the health visitor lady comes round to check on his progress.

Wednesday 31
Hallowe'en

Rachel Riley has thrown a pumpkin at Dean Denley.

Hurrah, it is Hallowe'en, ancient pagan festival and key date in my new Wicca-based calendar. Am utterly ready, i.e. have pentacle, black cloak (James's recycled Ninja cape) and have been practising my thirteen witch goals. Which is kind of like the Ten Commandments, but less about coveting oxen. I have completed five so far, i.e.

1. know yourself (duh);
2. know your craft (can remember at least one chant);
3. learn (am always learning, it is impossible not to under Mum's regime);
4. keep your words in good order (not sure if this is about reciting poetry or not swearing but am excellent at Kipling and have not said the B word for a day);

167

5. breathe and eat correctly (am always breathing and have eaten health-giving wholemeal toast and Manuka honey for breakfast, which is totally Wicca as bees are magical anti-bacterial ones).

Have still got several to go, including 'apply knowledge with wisdom' (no idea what this means), meditate (dog does not like humming noise), and achieve balance (fell off front wall trying to stand on one leg). But on plus side, am definitely going to out-Wicca Sad Ed. He has only done two. And his cape has a floral flock design as it is the bedspread from the Aled shrine room. We are meeting at Scarlet's after school and then we are going to have a solemn parade to the maze. (Labyrinths of all kinds are ancient mystical symbols with power seeping out of their pathways, according to Scarlet. Although we are waiting until trick or treating is over, as do not want ceremony disturbed by nine year olds in Batman outfits high on Swizzels and Um Bongo.) It is going to be excellent. James is also excited. He is foregoing trick or treating as he says he will be too busy hustling the souls of the dead as they all emerge from their burial grounds to wreak havoc on the living. He and Mad Harry are offering a mobile exorcism service. They have persuaded Dad to drive them around in the Passat (Mum has got Conversational French for the Over-40s). He has agreed on the grounds they are delusional and no one will ring them and he will be able to watch *Morse* repeats in peace.

They are mental. The financial rewards in trick or treating far outweigh exorcism. Mark Lambert made £56.70 one year and he didn't even have a costume. Although it may have involved menaces.

11 p.m.
Hallowe'en has been cancelled. It is because Scarlet is in a complete strop. Not only did neither of the Tamsins turn up, but, according to Scarlet, I am utterly unWiccalike and have compromised her channels of communication with middle earth. (It is because Barry the Blade appeared from behind the climbing frame (in his costume of choice—i.e. hairy tramp) and made me scream in terror.) I pointed out it wasn't entirely my fault as Scarlet was supposed to have brought frankincense or dragon's blood to purify the ground but Suzy didn't have either so she used half a bottle of Suzy's Merlot instead, which is not at all sacred. Sad Ed is in trouble as well. He was in charge of Wicca catering, i.e. mead and marigold custard (as recommended by Celestine Norton) as offerings to the Goddess. But he brought Shloer and butterscotch Angel Delight. Scarlet says she is thinking of ditching the coven and going back to normal gothness, as it is less fraught with potential failure. She called Bob and got him to pick her up in the Volvo and take her home so she can ask the runes what to do. He was dressed as Superman, with a Gordon Brown mask on top of his head. I asked him where the party was. He said, 'What party?'

Dad and James are still missing in action. Clearly Dad underestimated the number of potential paranormal emergencies in Saffron Walden and has been ferrying James and Mad Harry and their tools (ghostometer, Hoover, dog (who, they claim, can sniff weird things) around town all night). I wonder if they saw the Tamsins. Maybe something paranormal happened to them, i.e. they were sucked into a vortex and are now hovering above my head as I write.

6 Eggs

november

Thursday 1

Scarlet Stone has slapped Tamsin Bacon.

The Tamsins were not sucked into a vortex. They were busy being beguiled by Trevor Pledger's batlike charms on the bench outside Gayhomes. (Or rather Tamsin Bacon was. Tamsin Watts just watched and sucked a Chupa Chup.) It is all over school. According to one of the minigoths, Trevor has had his eye on Tamsin Bacon for weeks and gave her a Hallowe'en ultimatum to choose between him and the coven. Scarlet is mental with anti-sisterhood anger. She says it is a double betrayal as she taught Tamsin Bacon everything she knows about being a Goddess and now she is breaking vows with the bat boy, who is obviously only doing it to make her jealous and beg him to take her back. I am not so sure about this but Scarlet has declared open warfare with Trevor none the less. It is ultimatums all round as she has given Tamsin Watts until midday to decide who to sit with at lunch. She is going to try to lure some of the more impressionable minigoths as well with promises of Wiccan implements and communication with middle earth. I said that she said Wicca was not a weapon with which to meddle in the affairs of ex-lovers, but then she hit me with a Frube so I shut up.

12.30 p.m.
Scarlet is jubilant. It is not that she has been chosen by Tamsin (clearly she would rather eat yoghurt-covered

raisins while her best friend gropes bat boy). It is because she has acquired three apprentice goths, including Melody Bean who has a tarantula. Scarlet has made them sign up to our sisterhood Simple Life/witchcraft pact and given them instructions to get wands by next Monday. She made me and Ed renew our vows too. Have not told her about Hilary. Do not want to push her back over edge of post-Hallowe'en torture. A syndrome also being experienced by James. And Dad. It is not due to their failure to cleanse Saffron Walden of evil spirits. It is because Mum found out what they were up to and has quarantined the Hoover and banned Dad from going out for a fortnight. Only the dog is happy. It got five Crème Eggs and a Curly Wurly on its rounds last night despite failing to sniff anything weird.

* *

Friday 2

Scarlet Stone has jabbed Trevor Pledger in the eye. (This is not a Superpoke. This is actual.)

Scarlet is livid. Trevor has won back two of the minigoths. It is because he promised them they could play with his rats at the weekend. Plus Gemma Ellington said her boyfriend was worried the Simple Life vows would interfere with their sex life. (They are in Year 7. They do not have a sex life.) Also Trevor and Tamsin were all over each other in the custard queue at lunch. Even Sad Ed said it was putting him off his food. A feat that has not happened since he got gastroenteritis, and even then he managed a packet of Hula Hoops. I pointed out that at least we still had Melody Bean. This seemed to cheer Scarlet up a bit, as it means we have custody of the tarantula (Arthur). She has told Melody to bring it to coven on Sunday so we can absorb its supernatural powers. I hope she does not mean literally. I do not want to be consuming tarantula. Anyway she is a vegetarian so it would be illegal. She won't even eat barbecue beef Pringles.

Saturday 3

Ed Thomas is temporarily closed for refurbishment.

Am utterly disillusioned with the whole work ethic thing, i.e. I spend literally eight hours (minus lunch break minus two Fruesli and herbal tea breaks) slaving away every Saturday in the lentil-scented sweatshop yet my debt is still epic in proportion. According to Mum (who has subsumed all smaller debts, loan shark style, and is charging me interest at two per cent as a lesson in money management) I will not be debt-free until at least February next year. I said what about overtime in the holidays, but she says she has already taken that into account, as well as Christmas present money and WHSmith tokens, which she will exchange on a face value basis.

175

I pointed out that it is Christmas party season coming up and I have not had any new clothes since Granny Clegg let me keep the dead lady dresses. Plus Scarlet gets a clothing allowance of £200 a term to spend wherever she likes. Mum said she wore the same shoes for four years as a child. Granny Clegg just snipped the ends off so her toes could hang out. But then she relented and offered to take me to Gray Palmer and get me something sensible, and of her choice. Declined as will end up in knee length skirt and roomy cardigan. Not even Kate Moss could get away with that. At least Hilary understands me. It is because his parents are also strict and make him work for a living. Although admittedly Mrs Nuamah is not limited in her wardrobe choices to beige Marks and Spencer.

On plus side, Scarlet came into work today to hang out, i.e. hide behind the Frugrains to spy on Trevor and Tamsin Bacon who were picketing Goddard's for selling non-Hugh Fearnley-Whittingstall chickens. I said she should be pleased as she is utterly anti-chicken suffering but she says it is a hollow protest as Tamsin is only doing it to steal her vegetarianism as well as her boyfriend. It is a bit rich that Trevor is joining in anyway, considering his ambition is to drink human blood. Scarlet is jubilant despite having to watch Trevor fanging Tamsin's neck in front of the chops. It is because *a*) Tamsin Watts was not spectating—Scarlet says she will be at coven tomorrow for sure and will prove essential in our battle to hex Tamsin Bacon as she has inside info; *b*) Dean Denley swilled the protestors away with a bucket of Domestos and it has bleached their black karate slippers irreparably; and *c*) Rosamund made her a herbal poultice to banish negative energy.

Sunday 4

Ed Thomas has left 'The invisible hand of Morrissey touches me when I sleep'.

Ed Thomas has joined 'Morrissey lives in my wardrobe'.

Trevor has won the battle of the minions by three goths to one. Tamsin Watts failed to show up to coven today. Scarlet rang her but she says the pressure from Tamsin Bacon is too much, plus they have just bought matching ra-ra skirts and it would be a waste not to wear them to the lower school disco. Scarlet pointed out she was turning her back on the one true religion (i.e. Wicca) and that all her mystical powers will dissipate into the ether but Tamsin Watts says Tamsin Bacon is going to form a rival coven with bigger and better hexing powers. Then, to top everything, Jack came in eating peanuts out of the pentacle, which pushed Scarlet over the edge and she had to go and lie down in her bedroom with the lights out for two hours. Me and Sad Ed commandeered the pentacle and went back to his to practise throwing Mojos into it.

Monday 5

Scarlet was off school today sick. She says she has potential black death and has been hexed by the Tamsins in their rival coven. It is not black death, it is flu. But I am going round after school for an emergency Wicca ritual. Scarlet says it will reverse the hex and despatch it back whence it came. She has also instructed me to scout out potential coven members in the common room to boost our ranks and out-coven the other coven.

6 p.m.

Have not acquired any new coven members. Oona Rickets said no on the grounds that Sad Ed is involved and thus it is not a female caucus. I pointed out his utter lack of masculinity but she says a penis is a penis, whatever it's attached to. Then Fat Kylie disagreed and demanded to see aforementioned penis to compare it to 'Donkey' Dawson's to prove her point. At which point Sad Ed remembered he had double music and left very rapidly. Fat Kylie and Thin Kylie have also refused on the grounds they 'ain't no lezzers', and Emily Reeve declined on the grounds she had to feed Lola Lambert. There is no way I am asking Sophie Microwave Muffins. There is nothing mystical about her. Except her liking for supersized nipples. Scarlet said it did not matter anyway as she was feeling particularly potent thanks to Rosamund's herbal poultice so we burned a black candle in the Nigella soup pot and thought evil thoughts about

178

the Tamsins. Although I have to say some of thoughts were a bit distracted due to presence of Edna cleaning burnt cheese off the Smeg oven with a cake slice.

. . . .

Tuesday 6

Scarlet is still off school with black death. She has texted me with strict instructions to check the Tamsins at hourly intervals for signs of the reverse hex working. I said what sort of signs? She said hair loss or giant boils.

3 p.m.

Do not think the hex has worked. The Tamsins were both looking utterly normal (i.e. corpse-like) with no visible abcesses or loss of hair. Will tell her it is taking time to manifest itself. Will not tell her I saw Trevor draw a skull on Tamsin Bacon's left thigh during lunch. Do not want to upset her in her fragile state.

. . . .

Wednesday 7

Scarlet is back. She says she is hex-free and full of divine power (and Lemsip Max). Also she claims my reports on the rival coven are less than illuminating and she is clearly the only one with Wicca insight.

1 p.m.

Scarlet has been given an official warning by Mr Wilmott.

It is for stalking. She spent all first break following Tamsin Bacon around school in the hope of seeing her hair fall out. She would have got away with it if she hadn't tried to get into the same toilet cubicle. Mr Wilmott said under normal circumstances he would refer Scarlet to the school psychiatrist (aka Mental Morris) but that she is an exception to all rules (i.e. he is scared Suzy will steam into his office with her vast bosom and even vaster knowledge of education policy). Instead he has imposed a restraining order. She is not allowed within two metres of Tamsin Bacon until the end of term.

Anyway, I am too busy to be concerned with Scarlet's hexing. It is because Mr Slatter has announced an A Level Politics visit to the Houses of Parliament at the end of the month. Hugo Thorndyke (Con), evil MP for Saffron Walden and environs, is going to show us the corridors of power and infamous tea-room, where all the back-handers and sneaky deals are done. So am now in utter moral dilemma due to having still not told Mum about dropping French for made-up Mickey Mouse subject. Will ask James for advice. He is like Mum's mini-me and will be able to gauge her potential reaction.

7 p.m.
James says I have two options. I can either come clean and hope that my honesty will temper her anger and she will limit my punishment to being grounded for a month and paying for extracurricular French lessons on top of

my mounting debt. Or I can lie and pretend it is a visit to the French Institute. Have gone for option two. Will just bring back a postcard of Edith Piaf and some Orangina and she will be none the wiser.

. . . .

Thursday 8

Rachel Riley is Lisa Simpson.

Ed Thomas is Lilo Lil Simpson.

Scarlet is depressed. It is because her restraining order is causing issues at lunch. Tamsin Bacon measured the distance between Goth Corner Mark II and the Coven Table and it is only 187 cm. So Scarlet made us shunt the table thirteen centimetres to the right but then the maths geeks complained that we were 'cramping their style' (as if this is possible). So then we shunted forward instead but we accidentally crashed into the Criminals and Retards table and spilt Primark Donna's Yazoo all over Davey MacDonald's Hi-Tecs. And then all hell broke loose with the Dairylea Dunkables and Mrs Brain had to take cover behind the wholemeal pitta bread (tough and cheese-resistant). She is not blaming Scarlet though. She is blaming Jamie Oliver. She says he is the root cause of all school food problems. Mr Wilmott *is* blaming Scarlet however. She has got detention and is banned from the canteen for two days. She has to eat lunch in Mrs Leech's office. This is not a punishment. Mrs Leech is an endless source of gossip and Peak Frean biscuits. She will never want to be rehabilitated.

. . . .

Friday 9

Dean Denley has joined 'Midget cowboy wrestling'.

Mr Wilmott is going to regret his restraining order. Scarlet is already party to several snippets of staffroom gossip, thanks to Mrs Leech and her inability to guard secrets for longer than an hour. According to Scarlet:

- Miss Vicar is actually a man (although Mrs Leech got this off Mark Lambert so it is utterly unreliable);
- Cowpat Cheesmond is on Prozac (reliable, she has seen the bottle in among the chicken wormer);
- Mr Vaughan has done it in the stationery cupboard with Miss Mustard, which sounds like Cluedo, but is not. Miss Mustard is Bridget Mustard, aka the lab assistant aka locust monitor.

Also, James has got a spelling bee next week. Everyone had to pick a letter out of the hat and learn as many words from the dictionary as possible. It is so 'everyone has a chance to shine'. James has got T. Mad Harry has got Q. Which, frankly, seems unfair as there are only about ten Q words and there are billions of Ts. James says he does not mind. He is relishing the challenge. Also Nige says he is not concerned so much with results as with taking part. Mum is not in agreement. She says results are everything and correct spelling is the lynchpin of civilized society, along with punctuation and antibacterial cleansers. James said it is because she is a Tyrant. And Theoretically Teratoid.

- -

Saturday 10

Rachel Riley is Tantalized by Tetrahedrons.

Oh God. It is Scarlet's birthday on Monday and have nothing to give her, plus no money to buy anything. Am going to have to beg Mr Goldstein for credit and give her some incense sticks or something. Or maybe he has some out-of-date carob muffins. Will throw myself at his hunchlike mercy.

1 p.m.
Mr Goldstein is entirely unsympathetic. He says he does not give credit, not even to trusted staff members, (he did not say trusted, but I am sure he meant it) and that Rosamund had the last of their out-of-date mushroom pâté for her cat, Marjoram. There is nothing for it. Am going to have to search attic for more childish pottery that I can pass off as Wiccawear.

6 p.m.
The dog is getting confused with James's spelling bee

practice. It has just been told to Transmigrate to the Transmission Territory (i.e. go and watch telly on the sofa). I think it preferred it when James spoke Elvish. It was marginally more understandable. Even I am having trouble. Asked him if he wanted to come and scour the attic for priceless collectables but he said he was Too Tetchy to Tolerate Trangams. Told him he was a Tenuous Twit.

7 p.m.
Have found a jewel-encrusted eggcup (me), five collages of goat pictures (me), and a portrait of the queen (James). Will give Scarlet the eggcup and say it is a chalice.

7.15 p.m.
James says it is not the queen, it is Des Lynam. Mum was right. He has no artistic potential at all.

* *

Sunday 11
Remembrance Sunday

Rachel Riley is Transacting.

A terrible thing has happened. The coven has disbanded! It is because Scarlet says seventeen is too old for childish activity like witchcraft. Also her hex has not worked and Tamsin has not lost any hair or got boils. She has a new plan. She is going to flirt outrageously with Trevor and win him back, thus utterly destroying Tamsin Bacon. I said this was totally anti-Simple Life and broke all the rules of our platonic relationship pact. But Scarlet says she is not actually going to do 'It' with Trevor, she is just going to pretend she will, then kick him where it hurts (probably literally knowing her), and it is utterly feminist and strong woman. I am not at all sure this is true, but there is no arguing with Scarlet once she has set her mind on something. She is going to invite him to her party next Friday and wear outrageously revealing clothes. This is Suzy's preferred method of getting what she wants. It is almost 100 per cent reliable.

Am sad about the coven disbanding though. Not only is my eggcup/Wicca chalice birthday present now utterly irrelevant, but will have nothing to do on Sundays. James took pity on me and asked if I wanted to join Ghost Hustlers. I said I thought they had also disbanded (though not voluntarily but under Mum's instructions). James says it is now a covert operation. Anyway, I declined due to ghosts being made up. And then he started in on the T words again and called me Tiresome and Tacky so I left.

. . . .

Monday 12

Rachel Riley is Transpiring.

Got a lift to school with Jack again today. It is in honour of Scarlet's birthday. Asked Scarlet when she was starting

185

her driving lessons but she says she has refused Bob and Suzy's offer on the grounds that cars are evil and polluting and utterly non-Labour friendly. I notice she is happy to swan around town in Jack's Beetle and the vomit Volvo though.

Gave her the chalice anyway. Said it was an ironic eggcup. She said no it isn't. You made it in Mrs Barrow's class in Year Three. Luckily she was too busy with her campaign to win back Trevor to complain officially. She Superpoked him three times last night and 'accidentally' raked his green patch. It is lucky the coven has disbanded and we are back on the Alternative Music Club Table otherwise Trevor would have witnessed her doing unmentionable things with a Fruesli bar. As it is Dean Denley had to leave the table clutching his Incredibles lunchbox. (Not a euphemism. It is red plastic with a picture of Elastigirl on it.)

Tuesday 13

Scarlet Stone has sat courtside with Trevor Pledger.

It is James's spelling bee today. Thank God. So far this morning he has managed to get Tincture, Transgender, and Tickety-boo into conversation. Even Mum is finding it all a bit wearing. Also his mania for T words has revealed a few shortcomings in her own lexicon. I saw her having to look Totipalmate up in the OED after

Shreddies. (It means web-footed. She has claimed victory on the grounds it was used totally out of context.)

5 p.m.
Mum is writing to the council. It is because James came second in the spelling bee, even with ten out of ten. The victor was Maggot Mason, who won despite spelling 'calamity' with a k. It is because he has shown the greatest value-added improvement on last term (true, as he used to spell most words with a k). Mum says St Regina's is going the way of notorious anti-establishment establishment Summerhill, where pupils can choose not to attend lessons and are all too busy engaging in underage sex and binge drinking. I said this was taking it a bit far as, to my knowledge, there is no groping or alcoholism among the Year Sixes yet, but she says unmonitored spelling bees are the tip of the iceberg.

· ·

Wednesday 14
Scarlet's win back/harassment campaign of head bat boy Trevor is reaching new peaks. Today she wore her full length vegetarian leather coat over a corset and knee-high boots. I said I was amazed Suzy had let her leave the house like that. Jack said, *au contraire*, the corset is Suzy's, as is the whip.

In stark contrast, mother-daughter activity at Summerdale Road consisted of cleaning out the mung bean cultivator.

187

The dog had accidentally dropped a chipolata in it during one of its illegal forays onto the Formica worktop, and it was cultivating things besides healthy-giving beanshoots, i.e. health-compromising mould and some sort of jelly-like glue that James claimed was ectoplasm and demanded to save in a marmalade jar. He is wrong. Although it might be worth saving and sending to GCHQ as potential chemical weapon.

Also, Mum reminded me I am having a new brace fitted by sadistic Mrs Wong tomorrow. Admittedly, as am only having platonic relationships from now on, it is non-love life compromising. But will still be hideous again. Well, more hideous. Hair is always this mental. It is lucky am not doing French as all the cedillas would result in excess spitting and would fail any potential oral tests. In fact, she should be grateful am doing politics. Bad teeth are essential political wear.

. . . .

Thursday 15

Rachel Riley is speechless.

A miracle has occurred. Mrs Wong has refused to give me a brace. It is not because she has had sudden moment of clarity and given up sadism. It is because of NHS cutbacks. She says my problem is not severe enough to warrant free treatment and it will cost £350 if I want it done privately. Mum has refused on the grounds I am never going to be model material. Hurrah. Although am bit sad about the model thing. Said she should be blinded to the negative in her children. She said chance would be a fine thing. Thank God for New Labour's criminal underfunding of dentistry. Will text Scarlet to show support for this progressive policy.

· ·

Friday 16

Rachel Riley is Kate Nash.

Ed Thomas is Nashville, Tennessee.

Hurrah, it is Scarlet's party tonight. Though, obviously, it is purely going to be a celebration of music and laughter, now that sex and snogging are off the agenda. Me and Sad Ed have got our sleepover stuff ready (Morrissey T-shirt, toothbrush, copy of *Mojo*—Sad Ed; vintage silk pyjamas, entire make-up hoard, copy of *To Kill A Mockingbird*—me) and the common room is awash with anticipation. There are already rumours that she has secured the White Stripes as entertainment. This is not true. It is Duncan Evans and his CD player, as usual. Plus Jack is going to do an acoustic set. Although quite how you do an acoustic set on drums I am not sure. But there is only one invitee that Scarlet cares about, and that is infidel bat boy Trevor Pledger. Will he betray Tamsin Bacon and make an appearance, or is he ensnared in Tamsin's evil web of hexes?

189

3 a.m.

Apparently he is ensnared in Tamsin's web of hexes. Although Scarlet says it is not too late. She is waiting up until at least four in case he has got lost on the way or something. She is mental. Am going to bed as have to be fresh as a daisy for the lentil bins in less than six hours. There is no sign of Sad Ed. He was last seen at eleven when someone tried to shut him in the fridge. Jack offered to sweep the house but I do not think someone as gargantuan as Sad Ed requires forensic checking. He is either visible, or he is not in the house. But party has been success on Simple Life terms. Have snogged no one. And got complimented on silk (actually viscose and possibly not vintage as have 'do not tumble dry' label on them) pyjamas by Jack. He said I look like 1920s Evelyn Waugh heroine, i.e. out of *Brideshead Revisited*. See—it is utterly possible to be platonic with boys. Even ones you used to fancy.

3.15 a.m.

Unless he means *Vile Bodies*. Which does not sound very nice.

. . . .

Saturday 17

Jack Stone is.

Rachel Riley is not.

190

8 a.m.

Oh God. Have had two hours' sleep. It is due to Scarlet waking me up at five to ask whether I thought she should go round to Trevor's house and have it out with him. Answer—no, you mentalist, it is five in the morning, go to bed and channel some positive energy. Cannot believe have to be at work in an hour. Will beg Suzy to phone in sick for me. She is excellent liar.

8.10 a.m.

Suzy says she learnt her lesson the last time and is not double-crossing my mother again. Also to please not burst into the bedroom as Bob is always fruity in the morning. Left rapidly with eyes shielded from potential genital exposure. Will shower and eat Waitrose pain au chocolats. Am totally bound to feel better after that.

8.30 a.m.

Still feel horrible. Plus ate five pain au chocolats to combat low blood sugar and am now buzzing mentally. Cannot possibly walk five hundred yards into town. Am going to throw self at Jack's mercy and beg for lift in left-wing Beetle.

9 a.m.

Hurrah. Am back in bed with strong tea and T4. Jack utterly took pity on me and offered to do my shift. He is such good friend. Maybe he will even offer to give me his pay packet in order to alleviate third world debt. Possibly not. Anyway, can catch up on sleep, and *One Tree Hill*, and go home at 5.30 and Mum will be none the wiser.

9.15 a.m.
Unless she goes shopping for sesame snaps or other wholefood type fayre. Will call James and get him to divert her with suggested spring clean. That is like red rag to bull and she will be up to her elbows in Cillit Bang for hours.

6 p.m.
Hurrah. Am revived. It is not entirely due to day in bed watching *Veronica Mars* on Sky Plus with Scarlet, but is more in shock at James's terrifying new haircut, i.e. utterly bald. How can this have happened? Am going to interrogate Mum immediately.

7 p.m.
As always, it is O'Grady related. Apparently the Kylies came over and begged Mum to lend them James as a model for their hairdressing practice—they have a wet cut practical on Thursday. Mum agreed, on the grounds that they cannot do a worse job than Big Tony at Hair 2000, plus he was hindering her spring cleaning with his insistence at being in charge of hoovering (it is his new covert ghost detecting method). This was her crucial mistake. The Kylies can always do a worse job, no matter

192

how bad the alternative is. Anyway, James and the dog
came back from the Britchers' two hours later, with an
ASBO haircut, i.e. Mohican and a lightning flash shaved
into one side. (James, not the dog. Apparently it spent
two hours trying to mate Fiddy, despite having no
testicles.) Mum had complete panic and shaved him
completely with Dad's Gillette Mach 3 (the best a man
can get). So now he looks like nit-riddled Irish orphan
from *Angela's Ashes*. Mum says it is better than looking
like an O'Grady.

. . . .

Sunday 18

Have had thought. What has happened to Sad Ed?
According to Jack, who heard it off Dean Denley, who
heard it off Tracey Hughes (Waitrose tampon and
deodorant aisle, Mum answers phones at police station),
he did not show up for trolley herding duty yesterday.
What if he had sudden untimely death urges at Scarlet's
party and drove off in the sick-smelling Volvo and crashed
it into one of the many and perilous mini roundabouts?
Will pop over after Shreddies to check he is alive.

11 a.m.

He is alive. But shamefaced. It is because he got off with
Melody Bean at Scarlet's party on Saturday night. I
reminded him of our pact but he said the mind was
willing, but the flesh was weak. Also he had two bottles of

cider and his vision was impaired. On the plus side, he claims it was a sex thing (or snogging, as he says he passed out before they got to the pants bit) and he will not be pursuing a meaningful relationship with her on any level.

It is still an outrage though. What with Sad Ed's antics, and Scarlet's hot pursuit of Trevor, I am clearly the only one able to ignore my lustful urges and retain any sense of dignity or integrity.

4 p.m.
Oh my God. Hilary has got an interview for Cambridge in two weeks. Granny Clegg rang to ask Mum if he could stay with us for the weekend to acclimatize himself to upcountry ways! Hurrah.

5 p.m.
Except I do not fancy him. Am strong woman. With no urges whatsoever. Men are not responsible for my happiness. I am responsible for my happiness.

6 p.m.
Am still totally excited though.

· ·

Monday 19

Melody Bean has stroked Ed Thomas.

Jack picked me up for school again this morning. He said

he had excellent news to tell me. It is that he has got an interview for Cambridge in two weeks. I said it was indeed excellent, as he can take Hilary with him so he doesn't get lost. Then Jack remembered he had to collect Oona and made me get out at Mr Patel's.

School was good though. It is because Mr Wilmott has announced that, in lieu of a school play (all theatrical performances suspended after the lower school did *Jesus Christ Superstar* and Herod (Kyle O'Grady) had an impromptu bareknuckle fight with the apostles), we are going to have a charities week, utterly run by the Sixth Form. And Mr Vaughan. I said I was going to sign up for the slave auction but Scarlet has forbidden it on grounds of it being racist, sexist, and anti-workplace rights. She has banned the Kylies' charity *Swan* makeovers on the same grounds. Sad Ed is not signing up. It is in case Melody Bean tries to buy him. She is clearly not of the opinion that it was a sex thing and is aiming for a meaningful relationship. Sad Ed had to miss double English to avoid bumping into her on B Corridor. So it proves that not only does snogging compromise your happiness, but also your academic potential.

. . . .

Tuesday 20

Ed Thomas has joined 'Leona Lewis is not the future of music'.

Have signed up to be a slave. So has Scarlet. It is not because she has declared them racism- and sexism-free. It is because Tamsin Bacon has signed up and she is refusing to be outcharitied by her former protégée. Plus she will get to wear a revealing outfit on stage and potentially lure Trevor back into her clutches. Before she chucks him again. Even Sad Ed has relented. It is because Scarlet told him to. And he is more scared of her than Melody and her tarantula.

Wednesday 21

Rachel Riley is small, but imperfectly formed.

Mum is making us change all our bank accounts. It is yet another identity theft panic. This time it is not Facebook that is the culprit but mad-eyebrowed Chancellor Alistair Darling. He gave the entire country's child benefit records to a motorbike courier who has now lost them. I am unsurprised. Stacey O'Grady was a motorbike courier for a bit and he was always 'losing' stuff. Though it was usually DVDs, not tedious government documents. Mum now thinks rogue couriers will be hacking into Barclays and money laundering her millions. I said I only had £1.04 in my Post Office account so I do not think I am potentially at risk but she is not taking any chances. Dad is livid. He says he has only just sorted out the BT direct debit after three hours on the phone to some foreign call centre (it is in Cardiff).

Thursday 22

Sad Ed has been thrown back into the pit of despair. It is his driving lessons. Mike Wandering Hands says at this rate Sad Ed will be twenty-one before he is legally in charge of a vehicle. I said it was just psychological trick to make him work harder. But Sad Ed says he does not think so. It is more to do with the fact that he broke the faux walnut knob off the gearstick.

. . . .

Friday 23

Ed Thomas is young, gifted, and fat.

Hurrah. Have got new moneymaking scheme. It is not illegal drugs or prostitution. It is babysitting for my godson and uncle Baby Jesus. Grandpa and Treena are taking positive steps to improve their relationship, i.e. Treena is going to let Grandpa go with her down the Queen Elizabeth instead of making him stay at home while she mainlines Vodka Reef. I am going round this evening to enjoy free biscuits and Sky. In a responsible, child-friendly manner of course.

1 a.m.

Grandpa pays worse than Mr Goldstein. I have amassed a mere £10 for five hours of pure hell. Admittedly, I should have known better than to take the dog with me. But it eating the doormat is nothing compared to

197

Baby Jesus's unsociable habits. Treena is operating a free and easy bed routine, i.e. letting Jesus fall asleep in front of telly, whatever time that might be. (This is not down to baby whispering or any other Suzy-style weirdy stuff but is because otherwise he wails ceaselessly and bangs his head against his cot in a disturbing manner.) So had to put up with him until ten o'clock. He ate all the biscuits and refused to let me watch E4. Tried to instil some spiritual guidance in him, i.e. explain several deadly sins, including gluttony and not-sharing (not sure if this is one, but couldn't remember them all and there is no Bible at Harvey Road to check these matters) but his response was to stick a Cheerio up his nose and I had to get Mrs O'Grady from next door to suck it out with a curly-wurly straw (did not want to call Mum as she would ban me from baby-sitting for sure). Anyway, Mrs O'Grady is experienced in these things—she has raised at least nine children and most of them are alive. Then, it turns out there is a lock-in at the Queen Lizzie and so Grandpa and Treena did not get in until quarter to one and had spent all my pay on the fruit machine and Frazzles. Have got an IOU slip written on a barmat instead. Which is hardly legal currency. Will put it in Mum's debt collection box (a WHSmith petty-cash tin, locked, with keys stashed in unknown hidey hole). She is good at extorting payment out of Grandpa.

Saturday 24

Dean Denley has thrown confetti at Rachel Riley.

Oh my God. A groundbreaking and non-lentil based event has occurred at health food outlet Nuts In May. It is the presence of rock god and former meat mincer Justin within the taupe-stained walls. He came in just after Rosamund had finished showing me her new rash, to buy kelp tablets (to make his hair grow extra rock star long). But then he asked me if I wanted to go to his gig at the Bernard Evans Youth Centre next Saturday. I said yes. Well, actually, I said 'ggllhmmpph' as was eating one of Mr Goldstein's patented oatmeal and raisin bars at the time, but it's almost the same thing. Although I think he may have taken my red face and enthusiasm the wrong way because he said, 'Just as a friend. Sophie will be there. Bring Scarlet too if you want. And Jack.'

Hurrah, it is obvious he shares my platonic desires. Or else he is lacking friends. Or else he is utterly brilliant and wants to show off to his enemies. Whichever, I do not care. I am totally going. Though will not tell Scarlet yet. She is bound to take it the wrong way. Even though fact that I did not fall into heap under dried chick pea bins and weep inconsolably proves I am totally over him.

Unlike Dean 'the dwarf' Denley. The presence of his predecessor over the road sent him into a mincing frenzy. I think he is worried Mr Goddard may sack him and beg

Justin to come back. It is the height disadvantage. He has to stand on a chair to do any hacking.

. . . .

Sunday 25

Rachel Riley has tripped up Dean Denley.

Hurrah! Another brilliant Justin-related thing has happened. He has Facebook-friended me! Am overjoyed with Superpoke potential. Cannot decide whether to throw a sheep at him or challenge him to 'name that *Baywatch* babe'. Which one says 'I platonically like you and am utterly not going to try to get anywhere near your under-sized nipples despite fact that you are rock genius with good hair'?

4 p.m.
James has issued a Justin-related Facebook warning. He says he will be monitoring exchanges on an hourly basis and there will be penalties for breaches. Pointed out that he is banned from Facebook entirely. He said under Mum's terms he is banned from actually partaking of Facebook but she made no mention of not watching other people do it. He is a pest.

8 p.m.
Oh God. Just got a Facebook event invitation from Scarlet. It is an emergency meeting to discuss 'pact slippage', i.e.

she knows about Justin. Curse Facebook status updates. Cannot even keep my platonic relationships private any more.

9 p.m.
Jack has just hit me over the head with a diseased frog. (In the virtual sense, of course. The house is thankfully frog-free following the demise of Donatello, Michaelangelo, and Raphaelo at the hands, or claws, of the death chicken.) What is everyone's problem? I lit a menorah with Justin. Which is entirely non-sexual.

. . . .

Monday 26

Rachel Riley is blaming the dog.

Scarlet is going bonkers about the Justin thing. She says I am going to end up in Phase One again if I am not careful or, worse, in Phase Nought, i.e. back within his evil (but manly) arms. I said, *au contraire*, it is utterly Simple Life as it will prove once and for all that I am totally capable of platonic relationships, and is actually a forward-thinking step. Plus he is not evil. She said, yeah right. Then she pointed out that I can't go to the gig anyway as Hilary will be in residence and I will be too busy showing him cultural things. I said what could be more cultural than a guitar solo from a potential rock god. She said, 'What isn't?' Sad Ed is not so judgmental. Partly because there would be all sorts of pot calling kettle black issues due to his liaison with tarantula-loving poetess Melody Bean, plus he wants to go to the gig to see 'whether Justin's sound has evolved', i.e. he wants to beg to be in the band again.

Scarlet is mistaken anyway. I am utterly not interested in Justin in the non-platonic sense.

5 p.m.
Am I?

6 p.m.
No am not. As have Hilary as top platonic friend to resist and he is a trainee doctor which trumps being able to play 'Stairway to Heaven' any day. Have checked with James. It is official. Plus Jack is second in line to the non-platonic throne. Admittedly am not entirely sure he fancies me still, or that I fancy him, but he is still an excellent reserve as his car is left-wing and he can do a Johnny Cash impression.

- -

Tuesday 27

Scarlet Stone has joined 'I don't think the David Miliband on Facebook is the real David Miliband'.

Hurrah, it is the Politics A Level trip to the Houses of Parliament tomorrow. Scarlet has already drawn up a list of complaints to raise with Hugo Thorndyke, evil MP for Saffron Walden and environs. It is lucky Mr Slatter has not given Hugo a list of attendees or he would be changing his mind about educating the next generation in the ways of democracy immediately. He is a sworn enemy of the Stones ever since Suzy tried to smear him in his election campaign. Sad Ed is disappointed about not coming. Not because he wants to absorb the ancient atmosphere of the corridors of power. It is that he has double Art and is struggling with his gouache. Also it means he will utterly be at the mercy of Melody without me and Scarlet to protect him. I said it was all mind over matter. He said it is not his mind he is worried about. It is his penis. At which point I ended the discussion. James is also sad he is not coming. It is because the Houses of Parliament are allegedly stalked by no less than forty-three apparitions. He says Ghost Hustlers over the centuries have made pilgrimages to try to capture the fearsome 'bleeding Speaker' on camera. He has begged me to take pictures instead. Have agreed. Although will tell Mum they are French ghosts. She still thinks I am going to see *La Vie en Rose* sans subtitles.

. . . .

Wednesday 28

David Miliband is no longer friends with Scarlet Stone.

9 a.m.
Am utterly filled with potential political excitement. Have gone for an outfit that says 'I am quirky yet utterly democratic and will not start shouting about troops in Iraq at any point.' Scarlet has gone for militant EMO. A look that only says 'I will harass you about the war endlessly and possibly throw fetid fruit.' We are just waiting for Len Viceroy to show up in his new super-coach (the old one was too riddled with vomit smell and only had two gears). According to Mr Slatter it has an onboard toilet and drinks dispenser. Which will alleviate the usual hazard of losing several people at Junction 8 services when we stop for a wee and a can of Tango.

9.25 a.m.
Supercoach is not so super. Toilet is blocked after yesterday's Over-70s Horticultural Club outing to Peterborough and the drinks dispenser is a coolbox of Pepsi. Still, it does not matter as am too excited about seeing Gordon Brown shouting at some Tories to think about refreshments. Scarlet is already in trouble though. Mr Slatter did a bag check and made her remove half a dozen organic eggs and a flour-filled condom. It is for the best. Do not want anything else going wrong. Although, judging by previous school trips to the Paris Travotel and Davey MacDonald's swan-helmet ballet performance, the odds are not in our favour.

10 p.m.

As predicted, all did not go quite as smoothly as it might. It is Scarlet's fault. She has been banned for ever from the Houses of Parliament, and school outings, on the following grounds:

- trying to engage man-voiced Ruth Kelly in a discussion about VAT on tampons;
- trying to infiltrate the debate floor during a row about pineapple imports;
- trying to perform a citizen's arrest on Hugo Thorndyke for crimes against the working poor.

I have also been banned. It is not for political agitation. It is for spilling Monster Munch all over the political carpet. Plus my camera got confiscated by a man in tights. I pointed out I was in no way an evil Al Qaeda spy plotting to blow up the seat of government but he said 'rules is rules'. It is going to be sent back once they have checked it for incriminating evidence. Politicians are so out of date. It is lucky I had Scarlet's mobile phone with me.

· ·

Thursday 29

James has uploaded Scarlet's mobile phone photos onto his computer and is going through them with a fine-toothed comb (actually a magnifying glass and his ghostometer). So far he has found no evidence of bleeding apparitions. Although there is excellent evidence of Scarlet getting thwacked by Hugo Thorndyke's *Telegraph*.

. . . .

Friday 30
St Andrew's Day (Scotland)

Ed Thomas is wondering if spicy tomato crisps count towards his five a day.

Hurrah, Hilary arrives in less than twenty-four hours. It is utterly significant and groundbreaking for the Riley household. Even Mum thinks so. She is going on a special shopping trip for Hilary-friendly products. I have warned her not to fall prey to outdated media stereotypes, or indeed Grandpa Clegg stereotypes, but I fear this may have fallen on deaf ears. I definitely saw desiccated coconut on her shopping list. It is also just twenty-four hours until Justin's gig. Though am not getting hopes up. It is merely an observation. Am utterly resolved on Simple Life pact. Although the presence of both political and rock geniuses may send me over edge. It will be true test of mettle.

december

TURKEY

Saturday 1

Dean Denley has thrown Santa at Rachel Riley.

Rachel Riley has sent the Grinch after Dean Denley.

Cannot believe I have to go to work on such a momentous day. Have begged Jack to do my shift so that I can pace up and down the stairs in anticipation but he says he did not give up his job so that he can play bloody Buttons whenever I have random Prince Charmings to moon over. He is wrong. Hilary is totally not Prince Charming. He is far too intellectual for that. Anyway it is probably not jealousy but is just worry about Justin's gig tonight. Scarlet says he is coming to watch, though it is totally for business, not pleasure. He wants to make sure rock foundation does not upstage Music A Level. Scarlet is also coming on business reasons, i.e. to ensure I stay within pact confines. Plus I told her Trevor is going to be there. She is struggling in her bid to win him back. According to Melody Bean he has given Tamsin Bacon one of his pet rats. Scarlet said he is only doing it to make her jealous, as evidenced by the fact that the rat in question is 'Benson', who has one foot missing, and not king rat 'Hedges'. I agreed. Do not want to get her all riled up again.

6 p.m.
Oh hurrah! Hilary is here. He is actually right now on my sofa watching *News 24* with James and the dog. Mum is in

catering overdrive. As suspected, she offered him coconut macaroons. Thank God I warned her that he didn't like pineapples or our fridge would be full of Del Monte by now. As it is the tinned tomatoes have had to move to the cupboard under the stairs to make way for rice and kidney beans. James is also in overdrive. It is because Hilary knows more cunning facts than James. Apparently James tested him on heraldry for over an hour this afternoon and he only failed on one count (King Ethelred the Unready). The dog is not so happy. It is no longer the centre of any sort of attention. It tried to make up for it by singeing itself on the gas fire but only got a rolling of the eyes and a firm tutting. Mum does not shout in front of guests, unless they are related.

6.30 p.m.
Cherie and Thin Kylie have just been over on pretext of borrowing a cup of flour. This is utter lie. It is to ogle Hilary and his potential 'Donkey' Dawson area. Mum saw through their plan anyway and sent them packing. They should have asked to borrow some Kraft cheese slices. Everyone knows Cherie does not cook.

6.45 p.m.
Marjory has just been over. It was not on pretext of borrowing flour. Or Kraft cheese slices. It was in digital spyware panic that a dangerous youth was holding us hostage. She means Hilary. She spied him with her

binoculars from the landing window and assumed he was a cat burglar. Is it any wonder I am desperate to move to bohemian Camden with such provincial neighbours? Oh, how I long to dwell amongst the drug dealers and gangsters that Amy Winehouse gets to enjoy. It is so unfair. Thank God we are going out before Terry gets back from five-a-side and comes over to entertain us with his comedy Nigerian accent. I cannot wait until the gig. Nor can Hilary. It is because live music in Redruth is generally limited to Steeleye Span and someone called Bobby Helmet. Am wearing my ironic tiara so that I stand out in crowd. Do not want Justin to miss me. It is not that I want him to see Hilary and be utterly jealous. It is more so that he knows I am supporting him in our new platonic relationship. I hope Scarlet is not wearing her goth corset thingy. Do not want Hilary to get wrong impression and think that I consort with loose women. I really hope they get on. It is utterly important that my best friend is friends with my best platonic potential boyfriend type person.

1 a.m.
Hurrah, it has been a successful gig all round. Justin winked at me from the stage (so I am happy), but forgot several chords in his guitar solo and the words to 'Ruby' (so Jack is happy). Sad Ed has persuaded Justin to let him be their emergency roadie and third emergency keyboard player (so he is happy). And, even though Scarlet was wearing her corset, Hilary said it was the sign of someone confident in

211

her own skin and with her own political and religious ideals (so she is happy). In fact they hit it off brilliantly and Hilary is staying the night at hers so that they can continue their discussion on renationalizing the railways. Jack said I should come back too but Scarlet said I would just get bored. She is right. Plus Sad Ed got minty about having to walk home on his own and being potentially raped by Melody Bean (who spent entire evening flashing false purple eyelashes at him over a carton of Strawberry Ribena—doubly banned in our house as, even though it is stain-making, Ribena should be purple and blackcurrant flavour). Said he was idiot as girls cannot rape men. He said Tuesday managed it. Anyway, agreed in end on grounds it is totally a sisterhood thing to do as Hilary's theory on fiscal rules took Scarlet's mind off Trevor and Tamsin who were groping in the VIP area (the toddler room). Plus Bob and Suzy are far more multicultural and will not try to give him fried plantains (i.e. bananas as Waitrose is sorely lacking in exotica) for breakfast.

. . . .

Sunday 2

Dean Denley has thrown an elf at Rachel Riley.

Mum is not at all happy about Hilary defecting to the Stones. Nor is Granny Clegg who rang at half seven this morning to check that he is not homesick. As if. She is worried that Suzy may corrupt him with her lack of morals and abundance of sexual implements. She and

Suzy have never seen eye to eye. It is because Suzy thinks
sex is as important as breathing and Granny Clegg has not
done it since England won the world cup.

Anyway, I have been despatched to rescue Hilary and
repatriate him to 24 Summerdale Road in time for lunch
(non-racist lasagne, but with questionable tropical fruit
yoghurt for pudding). Hurrah, we will be able to spend
entire afternoon together listening to my vast (thirty-nine
CDs) music collection and discussing Zadie Smith (have
not actually read it yet but have Googled plot and know
the key bits).

2 p.m.
Hilary is back but is having a post-lunch power nap. It is
because he and Scarlet did not go to bed until four this
morning. I said was it Suzy and one of her all-night cheese
and yoga parties but Hilary said no, he and Scarlet had
been talking about Tibet and completely lost track of time.
Then I remembered that I need to prove my political
credentials so showed him the photo I took of Scarlet
getting thwacked by Hugo Thorndyke (Con), evil MP for
Saffron Walden and environs. He said it was brilliant and
totally subversive and that we should send it to the
Spectator as further evidence of Tory suppression. Have
posted it on Facebook instead. It has a far bigger and more
influential audience than the *Spectator*. Hope he finishes
nap soon as want to show him round important cultural
sights in Saffron Walden, e.g. Barry Island and Mr Patel's.

4 p.m.
Hilary is up but is shut in the spare room for pre-interview revision. James and the dog are both under strict instructions not to pester him under any circumstances. James argued that his in-depth questioning could prove the difference between success and failure for Hilary but Mum says she didn't think the medicine professors would be asking him 'True or False—horses can't be sick'. May just knock on door and see if he needs any brain-stimulating digestive biscuits though.

4.15 p.m.
Answer no. It is clear that he is single-minded in his efforts to join the ranks of geniuses that have thronged the refectory tables at Magdalene (not Maudlin as had previously thought) College and that nothing will distract him from his task.

4.30 p.m.
Hilary has gone round to Scarlet's house. She rang to say they were having Suzy's Labour Party activist friends round to dinner and the conversation might prove stimulating. I said I might find it stimulating too (i.e. I might find Hilary stimulating) but she said, 'No you won't, you will try to change the topic to Hilary Duff's hairdo and eat all the Kettle Chips as usual.' Which is possibly true. Anyway, he is going to stay the night and get a lift to Cambridge in the morning. Bob is going to take him and

Jack in the sick-smelling Volvo on his way to Addenbrookes. I suppose it makes utter sense, like Scarlet says. Mum is annoyed again though. She had made prawn jambalaya for tea.

10 p.m.
Although what if Hilary is not just stimulating Scarlet's mind but also her pant-covered areas?

10.15 p.m.
No, am being paranoid. Scarlet is paragon of virtue as far as pact goes. Even Trevor stuff was only ploy to get back at Tamsins, not actually man-based activity. How could I be so doubting? I am like that apostle whose name I can't remember.

10.30 p.m.
Doubting Thomas. That's it.

· ·

Monday 3
8 a.m.
Am utterly on tenterhooks. It is in sympathy with Hilary and his efforts to overcome his lowly birth (i.e. Cardiff) and join the university elite. Have texted Scarlet to check how he is holding up. She says he is doing well under Suzy's calming influence. Hope she has not given him any of her home remedies (i.e. Valium). Texted again to say to

give him kiss and good luck from me. She said, 'With pleasure.' Am not concerned. Will not be Doubting Riley. Am strong non-jealous woman.

8.15 a.m.
Jack texted to say 'THANKS 4 THINKING ABOUT ME. NOT.' He has definite overuse of sarcasm. It will curry no favour with the interviewers at Cambridge if he continues in that vein all day. Anyway have texted back to say, *au contraire*, was thinking of him, but assumed he could tell that, telepathically. It is not strictly true but Jack is easily placated.

8.17 a.m.
Got another text from Jack. WHATEVER. That boy is heading for failure. He is obviously too het up to concentrate. Unlike calm Hilary. Texted Scarlet to say maybe I should drop round before school to offer words of advice to both candidates but she says they are in capable hands and not to bother until after school. Said I would see her in double philosophy. She said 'Not likely.' She is going with Bob in the Volvo to be official bag carrier. Am still not Doubting though. Scarlet is my sister. Not actual, as there is no way Mum would have let abortionist Bob near her high-waisters, but in mind, and endeavour.

3.15 p.m.
Thank God school is over. Could not concentrate at all in philosophy, i.e. if you were stuck in a drifting hot air

balloon with a lawyer, a doctor, and a pilot etc., who would you chuck out first? Said would chuck out fireman on grounds there is a height requirement so he is bound to be biggest, but not sure there was one in there in first place. Anyway am going over immediately for full debriefing. And also to collect Hilary as Mum says Granny Clegg is going bonkers over the treachery and is threatening to come up to Saffron Walden herself to oversee matters. Also because she is worried as he told her it was an Oxbridge interview and she can't find Oxbridge on a map and thinks he may have been tricked by people traffickers or aliens.

6 p.m.

It is good news. Hilary says his opinions on the Hippocratic oath and euthanasia went down well with the forward-thinking faculty and that he is pretty sure of a place. Jack is also jubilant. It is because the woman who interviewed him had a poster of Billy Bragg on her wall so he says they spent the entire interview discussing the 'demise of agitpop'. I said it was clear why Magdalene beat Selwyn in *University Challenge*. Jack said, 'Whatever'. Anyway, Hilary is back in Summerdale Road for his final night. We are having risk-free fish and chips and Dad has set up his *Lovejoy* video collection. He says it will provide a unique insight into East Anglian life. He is mistaken. The only thing it will provide insight into is Ian McShane's criminal hairdo. It is like claiming *Doc Martin* is accurate portrayal of Cornwall. Although Granny Clegg is under mistaken belief that it is fly-on-the-wall documentary. She actually wants to move to non-existent Port Wenn so that Martin Clunes can attend to her many and varied ailments instead of Australian lady Dr Kimber. Have bagged place on sofa next to Hilary none the less. Will be able to point out places we can visit together once he is installed in hallowed halls of learning next year. Hurrah!

. . . .

Tuesday 4

Hilary Aneurin Bevan Nuamah has left the building.

9 a.m.
Hilary has gone. He left at half past eight with a tear in his eye and a Tupperware box of Marmite sandwiches. We all lined up outside the house to wave him on his way. Scarlet came over especially. As did Thin Kylie, Cherie, Marjory, and Mrs Hooton from number 21. He has totally won over the neighbourhood. Except Sad Ed who is annoyed because he said Morrissey was the acceptable face of bigotry. And the dog, who is annoyed because it has had no attention for several days now, despite destroying several Constable placemats and an entire McVities Jamaican Ginger Cake. It got shouted at as soon as Hilary's eco- and Labour-friendly Nissan Micra pulled away and is jubilant at being restored to its rightful place as resident menace.

218

Oh, I will miss Hilary. It is totally like Cherie says, he is a breath of fresh air in these parts (except without the panting and possible innuendo). Am going to beg to go to Cornwall for Christmas. Scarlet is in agreement. She says she will happily accompany us. She is such good friend.

4 p.m.
Mum says there is no way we are going to Granny Clegg's for Christmas. She is still recovering from 2002, the year of the partially frozen turkey drumsticks. Am undeterred though. Will have to think of cunning plan. Oooh, maybe Grandpa Clegg will herniate himself due to over-stimulation from the *Daily Mail* and need round-the-clock care. Hurrah. Will pray for illness and misfortune to befall Belleview. It is utterly in a good cause, after all.

. . . .

Wednesday 5

Rachel Riley is behind you! Oh no she isn't. Oh yes she is!

There is good news, Simple Life-wise. Scarlet is totally over Trevor and Tamsin. They were groping on the sheep field at lunch, which normally would have been a cue for Scarlet to discard some of her clothing and wander provocatively through the sheep poo, but instead she declared that she is not interested any more and Tamsin can have him. She says his arms are weedy and he is too obsessed with bats. Which I did point out to her a year ago, but love is blind. I

219

said it was good news that she is so committed to our pact of platonic love. But she got a text at that point and disappeared behind the bike sheds (formerly smokers' corner, now nicotine patch corner) to reply. It is probably from Edna the non-Filipina cleaner. Suzy gave her a mobile for her birthday and she has taken to texting people randomly to update them on domestic issues and her 'thought for the day'. Scarlet once got a text saying, 'GORDON KILLED BILL FOSSET'S RABBIT. WE SHOULD EAT MORE RABBITS. THEY IS BLOODY VERMINOUS.'

- -

Thursday 6

Ed Thomas joined the group 'Left-handed people are up themselves'.

Oh my God. The picture of Hugo Thorndyke, evil MP for Saffron Walden and environs, thwacking Scarlet over the head with a *Telegraph*, is on the front page of the *Herts and Essex Reporter*. The common room is mad with potential political agitation. Scarlet is being hailed as uber-left hero-ine of Twelve Hopwood-White. So am I. It is because the article credits me as the photographer. Whatever happened to journalistic integrity? I blame Alastair Campbell and his insistence on naming and shaming sources. Thank God Mum does not get the paper (on the grounds it concentrates far too much on Sawbridgeworth and the 'footballer belt'). She would be going mental with potential punishment as it breaks a legion of rules, not least doing politics A Level. Scarlet said she did offer the story to the *Walden Chronicle* but they turned it down. It is because the editor Deirdre Roberts's cousin is married to Hugo Thorndyke's sister. Or vice versa.

5 p.m.
It is all over. Mum has clawed her way through my web of deceit with her forensic abilities and proved that I lied about French. It is all Marjory's fault. She does not get the *Reporter* either but Dr Braithwaite (huge hands, lazy eye, bottle of whisky in desk drawer) does, and she was browsing through it while she was waiting to get her verruca frozen. I tried to deny any involvement but then Mum produced her trump card. Which was not actually a card but was my confiscated camera. It arrived home in this morning's post in a Houses of Parliament jiffy bag. Mum does not believe in privacy law and opens anything, regardless of whom it is addressed to, including next door's post, which arrives through our door with alarming regularity due to postman Beefy Clarke being dyslexic. And lazy.

Have been sent to room whilst Mum and James devise suitable punishment. I did point out that whole deception had been James's idea but he said he did it to test my resolve. He is sneak.

8 p.m.
Punishment has been decreed. It is one to one conversational

French lessons with Mum on Sunday mornings. It is potentially torturous. She speaks as slowly as she drives and her favoured topics are *'Je voudrais le potage, s'il vous plaît'* and *'Ma voiture est cassée'*.

• •

Friday 7

9 a.m.

Something terrible has occurred. Again. My Facebook account has mysteriously disappeared. And this time it cannot possibly be Bruce and his canine Bermuda Triangle. Scarlet has already texted to ask why I have not responded to her throwing a turkey at me at seven this morning. Told her that mysterious forces had swallowed my profile into the internet ether. She got all overexcited and said it was an evil Tory plot to censor free speech due to my candid Hugo Thorndyke shot. She is going to alert Hilary so they can mount a counter publicity campaign. I said she had done enough damage already, thank you. Anyway, she is wasting her time. Think it is just Mum and her faithful anti-free speech sidekick James.

4 p.m.

Was right. It is Mum and James. Tried to set up a pseudonym account, i.e. reviving my underused self-appointed nickname Ray Riley, but immediately door burst open and James came in accusing me of playing with fire and that if Mum catches me it will be curtains.

On-fire ones I presume. I said I was at risk of becoming a social pariah due to my inability to hurl random objects at my 'friends'. He said, *au contraire*, everyone will be bored with it in two months and will be using YouTube instead. He has already put video camera on his Christmas list. He is wrong anyway. Facebook will never fade away. I will just have to go quiet for a while then re-emerge, like metaphorical butterfly, beautiful and with extra Superpoke power. Plus can check what is happening online anyway as have worked out Sad Ed's password. It is Frobisher (i.e. his toy rabbit).

Saturday 8

It is bad enough only earning £19.95 a day without then having to post every last penny into Mum's Fort-Knox-style money collecting tin. Mum has offered to top it up with £5 a week if I take on more dog-related responsibilities but have declined. The dog only responds well to James. It is their shared love of all things hobbit. Have also declined suggestions of extra babysitting for Baby Jesus on the grounds that it is mentally depleting. James has begged to do it instead. He says he will happily drum some spiritual sense into him. He has more chance. He is morally superior in every way and can sing the books of the Bible off by heart. Mum has said no, on legal grounds, although I can tell she thinks it would be better. Even my own mother has no faith in me. Plus there was no sign of

Justin on the iron supplement aisle today. He is clearly being non-platonic somewhere with Sophie Microwave Muffins. According to Scarlet, who overheard Pippa Newbold telling Duncan Evans on the saggy sofa two days ago, they are going to get engaged as soon as they leave school. They are such a cliché. Thank God it is Sunday tomorrow. Traditional day of lounging around in bed until eleven then watching *T4* round Scarlet's whilst consuming vast quantities of Nigella recipe cakes.

• •

Sunday 9

8 a.m.

Or not. Have just been rudely awakened by Mum and her Conversational French toolkit, i.e. a set of Linguaphone tapes and a menu from La Poule au Pot in Sawston. She is making us start as soon as have consumed Shreddies (i.e. le cereal).

9 a.m.

Mum has confiscated Shreddies due to my new method of chewing each individual Shreddie twenty times. Pointed out it was for digestive purposes and had read about it in her hypochondriac's bible (aka Dr Le Fanu's *Book of Family Health*) but she was having none of it. James is joining us in readiness for fast-track French at St Gregory's Girls' next year. He is confidently expecting to be put straight into GCSE.

11.30 a.m.

Thank God that is over. Mum is far stricter than Mr Vaughan when it comes to conjugating verbs. And not making up words. James excelled though. He successfully used '*zut alors*' in a sentence and knew the French for carburettor. As a reward Mum is letting him have Mad Harry over for the afternoon. She will regret it. They are bound to try some illicit ghost hunting. James is convinced that Marjory is actually a bride of Dracula (she is not, she has slightly elongated canine teeth). He has been staking her out since last Monday.

5 p.m.

James and Mad Harry are in serious trouble. It is for throwing holy water at Marjory over the fence to 'see if she melted'. Also they were catapulting garlic cloves through the conservatory doors. Mum says enough is enough. The ghostometer has been confiscated and the *Usborne Guide to Ghost Hunting* is being returned to the library tomorrow. James says he does not mind. He has a new purpose in life. It is to become the owner of a circus of midget animals. He is of mistaken belief that he can make fortune from strapping monkeys in cowboy hats to the backs of Falabella ponies and getting them to jump over a string of obstacles. He is going to be in charge of finance and costumes while Mad Harry is going to be ringmaster. They are idiots.

Monday 10

Granny Clegg rang this morning. It was not to inform me she had developed a new fortune-telling body part or that Grandpa Clegg had burst his colon or anything else useful. It was to ask whether chickens are mammals (she and Grandpa Clegg have been rowing about this for two days apparently). But it is excellent anyway as have solved the absence of Hilary/ban on Cornwall conundrum and without the need to resort to ill/dying relatives. I have seized the day and invited the Cleggs to come here for Christmas instead. That way, Hilary can drive them in his Nissan Micra and stay the night so as to minimize motorway madness and crash potential. Granny Clegg thinks it is a brilliant idea. So does Grandpa Clegg. It is not so much at coming to visit his eldest (and cleanest) daughter and delightful grandchildren, more at being chauffered by Hilary. He thinks it is ultimate in his admission to the upper middle classes. He is fooling himself. He will never be granted admission. Not when he thinks vests are acceptable outer wear. Have not told Mum yet. Will be surprise Clegg reunion. She will be utterly over the moon.

Tuesday 11

Scarlet thinks the Hilary plan is excellent. She has even offered to put him up for the night if things are too overcrowded at Summerdale Road. I said that was very kind but that as we are just platonic friends, he can sleep in my bed with me. Scarlet says she will join us under the covers as it will totally be like Brownie camp. Or squatting. Agreed as it is totally sister-like/left-wing activity. Sad Ed wanted to come too but we said no. There is no way my John Lewis junior bed can take the weight. Plus Mum has banned him from sleepovers after his midnight feast in Year Eight in which he consumed the entire contents of her superior biscuit box. (Only brought out for guests. The rest of us are limited to digestives, HobNobs, and rich teas.)

Wednesday 12

School is awash with slave madness. Forty-three people have now signed up to be sold by Mr Wilmott and his charity gavel (i.e. a broken woodwork hammer) and he has had to close the list a week early for fear that there will be no one left to actually do the buying bit. Scarlet is boy-cotting it again now that she is no longer interested in bat boy. But she says she will still support me and Sad Ed in our quest for total submission. I said it was not total, i.e. there was no sex involved, but she says that is not what the Kylies say. They are under distinct impression that it is tantamount to minor prostitution. It is not a deterrent. It is the lure that has made them both sign up. Am having slight second thoughts though. Not about sex. As am totally committed to platonic pact and will explain that to whoever buys me. It is worry that no one will actually buy me. Or will go for 10p while Sophie Microwave Muffins secures £100 in a bidding war between Mr Vaughan and several of the PE staff (male and female). Although suppose at least will get more than Sad Ed. His general air of moroseness is not conducive to being useful manservant.

$\cdots\cdots\cdots\cdots\cdots\cdots\cdots\cdots$

Thursday 13

Granny Clegg rang again this morning to check whether or not she could bring Bruce. Have said yes on the more the merrier grounds. James is getting suspicious though. It is because I dived over the breakfast table to grab phone before he could answer (luckily Mum was cleaning up dog-related mess on the downstairs loo door at the time). He says he hopes I am not plotting anything. I said people in glass houses should not throw stones. It is because I have seen his plans for the midget circus and they include harvesting fleas from the dog.

$\cdots\cdots\cdots\cdots\cdots\cdots\cdots\cdots$

Friday 14

Cherie has just been over offering Mum the 'night of her life'. It was a spare ticket to see the Spice Girls reunion concert. Clearly Cherie does not know Mum very well. The night of Mum's life would involve Jeremy Paxman and some Dettol. Cherie is going to ask Suzy instead. She is totally pro Spice Girls due to their girl power message.

Plus she is hoping to get Victoria Beckham on her celebrity sex sofa soon. She is desperate to gauge the actual proportions of David's willy.

· ·

Saturday 15

Oh joy. Another day with Rosamund and her many complaints. The only positive thing I can say about the world of lentil retailing is that at least I am not stuck outside in the harsh elements like Sad Ed who spent the day herding trolleys in a criminally thin polyester overall. He claims he now has frostbite and trolley foot (invented workplace injury caused by moronic dog-food eating supervisor repeatedly running over one's feet with a train of trolleys to see how many it is possible to endure without bones actually breaking). He actually asked if there were any vacancies at Nuts In May. He must be desperate. Sad Ed does not engage with wholefood unless it is emergency.

· ·

Sunday 16

Oh God. Cannot do any more conversational French with Mum. She is punishing me for failing at my punishment now. It is because she made me book a single hotel room with an en suite shower and I apparently asked for a wet double. Plus I forgot to demand a cursory check of the toilet facilities. James said he is stunned that I managed a

229

B at GCSE and it is just further proof that exams are not worth the paper they are printed on these days. James is in trouble too though. It is not his French (which is freakishly advanced). It is because he and Mad Harry 'borrowed' one of Marjory's guinea pigs for the midget circus and it is now lodged under the fridge with the dog going bonkers around the kitchen. She is regretting confiscating the ghostometer, I can tell.

. . . .

Monday 17

Hurrah, it is Charities week. Activities today are:

- Year Seven toasted sandwich lunch stall. (Brevilles encrusted with the remains of last year's Sports Day groundbreaking charity marshmallow and banana combo. So Mrs Brain not too in danger of being put out of business.)

- Throw wet sponges at a teacher (Miss Vicar and Miss Beadle). All sponges have been quality checked for hidden weapons after Darryl Stamp concealed pointy Yu-Gi-Oh toys inside them at the summer fete three years ago.

- Criminals and Retards sponsored silence. This is doomed to failure. But they have been banned from sponsored walks, sponsored swims, and sponsored transferring Rice Krispies from one bowl to another using only a straw and the power of suction, so this is the last resort.

Plus Mr Wilmott has announced that the end of term disco on Friday will continue in the slave vein and be a toga party. He is making a colossal mistake. Togas have too many access points. The Kylies will be pregnant by 9 p.m.

. . . .

Tuesday 18

Mum is agitated. At first thought she may have guessed secret Clegg Christmas plans but it turns out that it is just James's non-nativity at St Regina's. Nige has instigated a no-faith embracing celebratory talent show concert, complete with an opt-out policy for anyone who would rather string coloured pasta together instead. He says it will be less stressful for parents and pupils. Mum is not in agreement. The veins on her forehead are particularly bulgy. It is fear at James's role. He has refused to divulge the nature of his performance but he has gone to school in his leotard.

There is trouble at John Major High as well. It is not nativities. (They got banned several years ago after Suzy's temporarily successful campaign to portray the realities of childbirth complete with screaming and fake blood.) It is the BTEC hair and beauty *Swan* makeovers tomorrow. Only three people have signed up: underage O'Grady menace Kyle, his chavette-in-training girlfriend Primark Donna, and Mark Lambert. (On the grounds there is not much you can do with a skinhead. He is wrong. They will

231

wax him within an inch of his life.) Mr Wilmott has now changed the rules so that you can pay £10 and nominate someone for it instead. It is a stroke of genius. There has been a flurry of enemy-nominating activity at the upper school notice board and rumours abound (via the Maths Club gambling ring) that they have already raised £170. They are taking bets on who will look the worst. Odds are on Cowpat Cheesmond (gigantic beard with concealed food, lingering smell of manure, nominated by the Year Nine Criminals and Retards for not letting them kill chickens last Tuesday). I hope Sophie Microwave Muffins does not nominate me. I have already suffered at the hands of their grooming incompetence. My eyebrows are only just back to their unkempt selves. Oooh. Maybe I could nominate her though. Will ask Mum if I can borrow £10 for a good cause when I get home.

5 p.m.
Mum is not in a mood for handing out money to any causes. It is the no-faith celebration at St Regina's. It did not go entirely to plan and James and Mad Harry managed to lose all the school gerbils. Their act involved making the gerbils run around James's leotard while he did his scary dancing.

. . . .

Wednesday 19
Oh my God. There has been an incredible *Swan*

232

makeover-related event. It is malodorous bisexual Head Girl Oona with the hairy armpits (nominated by the entire common room on smell grounds). She has been Kylied and is fully waxed (including a particularly tricky bikini line, according to the Maths Club), deodorized and has had her hair dyed brunette (it was supposed to be bur-gundy but Fat Kylie used the wrong packets, as usual). But Fat Kylie's mistake is Oona's gain as she looks utterly stunning. Ooh, maybe am lesbian after all. It would be ultimate in Simple Life anti-men activity. And last efforts were somewhat half-hearted, i.e. only tried for two hours and was distracted by visions of Fat Kylie's minky. Yes. That is it! Am going to be lesbian. Possibly. Will not tell Scarlet and Sad Ed yet though. Saw Sad Ed looking somewhat non-platonically at Oona Mark 2 and do not want him as love rival. Although I would totally win on thin upper arms and breast grounds. Scarlet is a different matter though. She has excellent lesbian credentials including a KD Lang CD and access to vibrators.

Thursday 20

Hurrah, it is the John Major High first inaugural Charity Slave Auction. Am wearing Brownies T-shirt and miniskirt, an outfit that says I am willing and able to do my best, but not as willing as either of the Kylies. Plus Brownies T-shirt shows an interest in all-girl activity i.e. Oona will purchase me for potential lesbian discussions.

Sad Ed is wearing a waffle jumper and beanie hat. He will be lucky to get any bids at all.

5 p.m.
Have not been bought by Oona. In fact, she did not bid for me at all. Instead have been bought for a meagre £4.50 by Jack. And was not exactly frenzied bidding war. In end only he and Dean 'the dwarf' Denley stuck their hands up. Thank God Jack took pity on me to save me from the idiotic mincing midget. Although am disappointed at the Dwarf putting such a low price on love. £4.40 is hardly inspiring. He could get Leanne Jones to do him in a phone box for less.

In contrast, Sad Ed went for £28 after a three-way fight between Oona, poetess stalker Melody Bean, and Mark Lambert. Oona won. Obviously she wants him for some heavy duty carrying work. Sad Ed is delighted. And relieved. Mark Lambert was going to make him dance naked in the long jump pit (aka cat toilet). Slavery takes place tomorrow. We are at the mercy of our masters for a full six and a half hours, plus after-school activity by prior arrangement and an extra cost of £2.50 an hour. Maybe could charge Jack privately to alleviate my debt. Would be excellent PA type person, i.e. I look excellent in pencil skirts. Plus could be like Alastair Campbell and advise him on which outfit to go for to impress his electorate. Will ask him tomorrow.

Friday 21

4 p.m.

Have surprisingly excellent day as Jack's 'slave'. He and Oona were doing a common room Christmas makeover (which explains the purchase of Sad Ed for saggy sofa moving services). So just had to help him scrape all the Blu-tack (aka chewing gum) stuck to the walls and paint out the mural of dying Iraqis in front of Tony Blair in a devil suit left by last year's A Level Art group. It is in preparation for the next cohort of wannabe Tracey Emins. Do not know why we are bothering though. It is bound to be something equally clichéd. Jack turned down my offer of extra-curricular slavery though. He says it is bad enough having Edna trying to make him wear weird clothing combinations without me doing it too. He is so ungrateful. Edna is only doing it because she forgets where she has put half the washing, or else dyes it all yellow. He did offer to escort me to tonight's toga party instead. I said no, as I will be too busy being a lesbian with glamorous Oona. He said, 'There is no way you are gay, Riley. And I should know.' Which is possibly true as he has 'tested the goods' so to speak, and they did respond. But am not going to let him out-left-wing me. I can be gay if I want. And will show him tonight. Though will have to contend with Sad Ed. He is jubilant after a day spent cleaning the sofa with Oona (findings £3.80, four condoms, and a packet of custard creams). I reminded him of his no-sex with the opposite sex pact but he said

Oona doesn't count as she is a lesbian. He has no chance anyway. He has had to borrow one of his mum's superking pink polyester Argos sheets for his toga and it is still quite gapey around the manboob area. Whereas I am in John Lewis 200-thread-count Egyptian cotton (queen size), which is far more lesbian-friendly. Scarlet is wearing black satin. So will have to keep close eye on her.

12 midnight

Am not lesbian. At least not yet. It is because Oona did not come to the toga party due to having a prior anti-Taliban clothes swap in Harlow. Why did I not think to check these things? So had to slow dance to whingeing James Blunt with Jack. He said it was part of my duties as a slave. I pointed out that he hadn't paid his extra £2.50 but he said, *au contraire*, he had slipped Mr Wilmott a fiver behind Goth Corner Mark I. Think this is a lie. Agreed as it is Christmas after all. And is good that he would pay so much for a dance with me. Plus it was actually quite pleasant. He smells nice and his arms are deceptively strong. Ooh, maybe do still fancy him after all. Even though he has a penis and is not gay.

12.15 a.m.

No. That is not Simple Life at all. Especially as Scarlet is my sister which makes Jack my brother which makes it practically incest. Am definitely committed potential lesbian.

Saturday 22

Oh God. Have just realized that have not done any shopping and have only got three days to go until Christmas, one of which will be spent hawking lentils, one of which the shops do not open (except for Mr Patel's porn, junk food, and nicotine patch emporium), and one of which will be spent making merriment at the giant Clegg reunion so will too busy heating Fray Bentos and pouring Stones Ginger Wine to leave the house. Plus, have no idea what to get anyone and utterly no money with which to do it. In contrast, James has saved £56 and has drawn up a shopping schedule and options for every recipient in case WHSmith has sold out of his favoured items. Begged him to lend me some money and do the choosing and buying (which is the sort of responsibility he would have leapt at under normal circumstances) but he said he needs every last penny for the circus. On plus side he had an alternative suggestion. It is to do my shopping at Nuts In May using today's wages, before Mum commandeers them for the petty cash debt tin. It is genius.

6 p.m.

Not a brilliantly successful day on several counts. Firstly, had underanticipated wealth of Christmas-type goods on offer at Nuts In May so gift list is now as follows:

- Mum—additive-free sanitary towels (to show I do not think she is anywhere near being menopausal, she will be thrilled);

- Dad—CD of calming pan pipes (to play in car as radio is still stuck on Kiss FM after Bruce ate the tuning knob);
- James—sesame snaps (his snack of choice);
- Scarlet—Vitamin D capsules (to combat hours spent in darkened bedroom during goth phase);
- Sad Ed—box of creatine (so he can convert manboobs into muscle);
- Baby Jesus—beetroot crisps (will say they are 'special purple Skips');
- Grandpa—giant jar of omega 3 fish oil for brain power and joint lubrication;
- Treena—giant tube of organic KY jelly for actual lubrication;
- Dog—four packets of Linda McCartney sausages (it will eat real cardboard so these will be breeze);
- Cleggs—nothing. (They do not believe in wholefood, vitamins, vegetarian products, or anything wheat-free. Christmas with me will be present enough.)

Secondly, Justin came in. It was not for more kelp tablets (hair now approaching undersized nipple line). It was to 'collect his Christmas kiss'. I said I thought he was getting engaged to Sophie Microwave Muffins. He said, 'Not any more, she came on yesterday.' So I said I couldn't do it then and there due to a no fraternizing at work rule but that I'd think about it. He said, 'Cool, well, pop over on New Year's Eve and I'll give you one while Sophie's in the bog.' So am now in platonic Simple Life quandary. On the one hand, he is my two-timing ex, and is going out with someone else, so it would be utterly unsisterly and evil. On the other, he is gorgeous, she is a cow, and I am an utter lesbian in training, so where's the problem?

Thirdly, Rosamund is on a root vegetable diet and it is having a bad effect on her digestion. Mr Goldstein had to put her on stockroom duty as the smell was putting customers off their purchases. He is obviously immune to the usual odour of decaying vegetation that pervades his store.

But am festive none the less as tomorrow Granny and Grandpa Clegg will be here for the secret reunion. Which means Hilary will be here. Hurrah! Am going to spend entire morning making sure Mum is in excellent mood as do not want to spoil events for her.

Sunday 23
11 a.m.
Plan already foiled. It is entirely James and Mad Harry's fault. Mum found them making the dog jump over a series of obstacles in the back garden (i.e. her Vileda supermop collection, suspended on the patio chairs). Which would not have been so bad except that they had strapped Baby Jesus to his back. Mum has gone mad and has banned any midget circus activity. She has also banned Grandpa from the house for the rest of the day. He was encouraging the

whole proceedings. At least his presence will not incense the Cleggs. They have still not resolved the Terry Wogan greatest living presenter/annoying twat row.

4 p.m.
Where is Hilary? He left at least six hours ago, according to Scarlet who ate virtual figgy pudding with him at half seven. She is already here with her overnight bag for our three-in-a-bed platonic sleepover.

5 p.m.
Still no sign. And Mum has demanded to know why we are watching the driveway with James's binoculars. She says it is bad enough having one amateur private eye on the road without us jumping on Marjory's idiotic bandwagon. Said we were observing festive robins at play.

6 p.m.
The Cleggs and their plethora of Spar bags are here! And with them is their chauffeur Hilary. Hurrah! The delay was caused by an overturned Bernard Matthews lorry on the M11, complicated by both carriageways stopping to do some seasonal looting. They are settled on the sofa with two bottles of Mackesons and *You've Been Framed*. On the down side, Hilary has gone home as he has a crucial Christingle service tomorrow. Scarlet said he could go with her to the one at St Regina's. So I pointed out that she is anti all

240

religion on the grounds that it is the opium of the masses but she said she has had a rethink and it is utterly New Labour to be religious fanatic and uber left-wing, look at mad Catholic Ruth Kelly. Hilary said no anyway, as he is in charge of handing out oranges. But he is going to stay the night when he picks the Cleggs up instead. Mum asked when that might be. Granny said next Monday. Hurrah, so Hilary will be here for New Year. Plus we can enjoy a multigenerational family Christmas for a whole week. Mum is now having a lie down in her bedroom. I think she is overcome with joy at their surprise festive arrival. She has barely been able to utter a word. Except, 'Colin, fetch a J-cloth,' when Bruce weed on the lino. Dad has mopped up and is now at Waitrose with James, shopping for emergency Fray Bentos and a bulk pack of Andrex. He is dropping Scarlet off on the way. I said Hilary's absence was no reason for her not to feel at home in the arms of the Clegg reunion but she says Harry Hill brings her out in a rash.

10 p.m.

Entire house has gone to bed with festive Clegg exhaustion. In fact, Mum has not actually left hers since the lie down earlier. Dad was in charge of tea. Which was surprisingly good, i.e. proscribed steak and ale pie and Ben and Jerry's mini pots (Waitrose does not stock Viennetta). On down side, have got dog in my room. It is to prevent any Bruce versus Dog kerfuffle in the night. They have already established rival lairs. The dog has got the kitchen and the sofa and Bruce has got Granny Clegg's chair and the downstairs loo.

. . . .

Monday 24

Christmas Eve

10 a.m.

Mum is back with a vengeance. And not to my advantage. Have been ordered to take Cleggs on pilgrimage to Cromwell Road Spar as punishment for surprise reunion. It is to give Mum time to adjust all her military style festive catering and entertainment arrangements. James is aiding her with his highlighters and Tippex. Dad is avoiding all responsibility by going to work for his office Christmas lunch. He is under strict instructions not to consume alcohol in any quantity whatsoever. Mum says she will need all the backing she can get over the next forty-eight hours. James pointed out that actually she had the Cleggs for the next 192 hours, at which point Mum decided she needed another lie down. I do not understand her concern. It is Christmas, what could possibly go wrong?

3 p.m.

Have lost Cleggs. It is utterly not my fault. It is because Bruce got shouted at in the Spar by Mrs Overton behind the till for eating two cob rolls, so Grandpa Clegg shouted at Mrs Overton because apparently Maureen in the Spar at St Slaughter lets him do it all the time. Then Granny shouted at Grandpa for shouting and Bruce ran off in the hoo-ha with the Cleggs in hot pursuit. They were last seen heading down Peaslands Road towards the Lord Butler Leisure Centre. Mum is mental with concern. Not at their safety but at the possibility of them doing something idiotic to bring shame on the Saffron Walden wing of the family. Have been despatched with James to bring them home. Mum has ordered Dad back from lunch as well. She says she cannot cope single-handedly. This is stop press news as normally Dad does not get a look in when it comes to household management of any sort due to his habit of not sticking rigidly to Mum's many and varied systems.

5 p.m.
The Cleggs are back. James found them. They were round at the Britchers' having a Bruce and Fiddy reunion. He was alerted by the sound of 'comedy' Indian accents coming from the lounge window. Mum is livid. I said she should be happy that they are safe and have not embarrassed themselves or us, but she says they have spoiled their tea by eating two bags of frozen sausage rolls and a jar of cocktail onions. There is no pleasing some people. Also Mum is mad because there is still no sign of Dad. Hope he has not been caught in hideous pre-Christmas snarl-up on the A11 and is lying bleeding in a ditch somewhere.

6 p.m.
Dad is back. Was not bleeding in ditch. Was slumped in

back of Malcolm from IT's Honda Civic having consumed four glasses of Le Piat D'Or. (Which, allegedly, the French adore, though saw no evidence of this in St Abbatage. They were all too busy on the vile aniseed ball-flavoured pastis.) Mum has sent him to his room with a bottle of Evian and four pounds of potatoes to peel. It is a harsh punishment. Though necessary due to impending gigantic festive Clegg/Riley lunch. Mum is doing all the preparation tonight. The turkey is defrosting in the bath, James is doing the crosses in the sprouts and I am on foil cutting. Which is, according to James, statistically the hardest job to mess up. It means I am unable to attend midnight mass (actually at eleven and actually mostly involving drinking Bacardi Breezers in the back pews and singing too loudly in 'Hark the Herald') but do not mind. Tomorrow is a milestone in Anglo-Cornish relations and am eagerly anticipating Clegg and Riley barriers being broken down and everyone linking arms to sing festive favourites. (Except James who has an aversion to Band Aid. It is the line about snow in Africa. Which is apparently inaccurate as Morocco does, occasionally, enjoy icy conditions). Mum is worrying over nothing. It will be brilliant. I know it.

Tuesday 25

Christmas Day (i.e. Jesus's birthday in all senses)
7 a.m.
A terrible thing has happened. The Clegg/Riley peacemaking

Christmas lunch has been cancelled. It is not the Wogan argument rearing its ugly head, it is Bruce and the Dog rearing theirs. They have eaten ten pounds of semi-defrosted turkey between them, and a saucepan full of sprouts. Clearly they broke into the bathroom and kitchen in the night, working as one gigantic all-consuming canine force. Mum is lying on the bed with James wafting her with a fan (actually a copy of *Good Housekeeping*, how ironic) to revive her. Dad says not to panic as we can emergency defrost some other meat for lunch instead. But James pointed out that there is no other meat in the freezer due to gargantuan size of turkey so it is potatoes and bread sauce all round unless Mr Patel has branched out into organic poultry. He has not. He does not need to with his expanding nicotine patch empire. Dad says it is partially my fault as I was on dog duty in the night. I said it is not my fault that it has developed a freakish ability to chew handles off doors silently and anyway what about Bruce, i.e. it is Granny Clegg's fault. But Granny Clegg says Bruce got thirsty in the night so she let him out to go to the toilet and it is Mum's fault for putting a turkey in the bath. Cannot believe Granny Clegg lets Bruce drink toilet water. Especially Mum's. It is blue and infused with two kinds of Harpic. No wonder Bruce is troubled. Both the dogs have been banished to the back garden. It is not so much punishment as to avoid inevitable turkey and sprout vomit on carpet incidents. I said to Mum to look on the plus side, i.e. Grandpa and Treena are taking Baby Jesus round to her cousin Donna's instead so that is three fewer fussy eaters to cater for. She just stared glassily at the ceiling while James did extra frenetic wafting. Need to think of festive rescue plan, and fast.

11.30 a.m.
Have had genius idea. We can eat the dog's Christmas present for lunch i.e. the Linda McCartney sausages. Hurrah, have retrieved them from bottom of freezer and put the oven on. I, Rachel Riley, am single-handedly saving Christmas. Is totally like *Christmas Carol* when Scrooge shows up with a turkey for Bob Cratchit and the one with the crutches. I am metaphorical Ebenezer and my vegetarian sausages are a symbolic bond of friendship across a divide.

1 p.m.
Grandpa Clegg does not like his sausages. He says they are suspiciously gristle-free. I said they are also meat-free. He went pale and had to leave the room. It is his strict anti-vegetarian stance. Granny Clegg is more forward-thinking. She just drenched hers in Bisto. She said the claggy texture was quite pleasant. On plus side, feast has revived Mum slightly and she has agreed that present opening can go ahead at 2 p.m.

4 p.m.
Normality reigns once more, i.e. have had usual

unsatisfactory haul of Christmas gifts from relatives:

- Black baseball boots (Mum and Dad, but not Converse, actually from Clarks and, therefore, utterly unwearable);
- *Little House on the Prairie* (James, he said it is the ultimate Simple Life);
- Kendal Mint Cake (the dog, and not actually cake, as James pointed out);
- Cats of the World calendar (Granny and Grandpa Clegg, March missing);
- Brazil nut toffee (Bruce, 99p Trago Mills price sticker on bottom).

Apparently Dad wanted to write off my debt as a present but Mum pointed out that I would not have learned my lesson and would spend the rest of my life assuming I can rack up credit card bills and that they will happily sign cheques for me. I said I would utterly not assume that that is the case and had learned my debt lesson, but then James pointed out that, statistically, this is unlikely, and deprivation is really the only way forward. I said that it was their fault that their Christmas gifts from me were so ungenerous then, but it turns out that the Nuts In May presents went down quite well. James has already eaten all his sesame snaps and is now doing expressive dance to Dad's calming pan pipes CD. Mum was especially pleased with her sanitary towels, which she said were 'practical' (this is her highest form of praise). It is shame we ate the dog's sausages though. Have given him and Bruce some of my Brazil nut toffee to make up for it. (They are back in the house, albeit within the confines of the wipe-clean kitchen lino.)

7 p.m.
Dog and Bruce are unusually quiet. Mum says their co-operation is a pleasant surprise. It is also pleasant surprise that she is utterly back to normal, i.e. Cillit Banging every available surface and swooping with coasters before any beverage hits a wooden surface. It is because Christmas and its inherent chaos is over (Boxing Day does not count in her book) and she can go back to her normal frugal and hygienic regime.

7.15 p.m.
Christmas chaos is not over. It turns out that the dog's and Bruce's silence was not by choice. It is the Cleggs' Trago Mills Brazil nut toffee. It has glued their jaws together. Mum says they can jolly well stay like that until tomorrow as they have already eaten enough for a week. But Granny Clegg is worried Bruce might suffocate as he has excess mucus, so James is trying to prise his teeth apart with a spatula. Am going to retire to my room and revive self with tales of Simple Life exploits in *Little House on the Prairie*. Modern life is far too fraught for me.

· ·

Wednesday 26
Boxing Day

The dogs are still stuck. James is now trying to reheat the toffee to melting point with Mum's hairdryer. But all that is happening is that the dogs are getting voluminous hairdos. Mum has called Mr Mercer the vet for an emergency appointment. He says he will do it, but he is charging double as it is a bank holiday. Dad has agreed to foot the bill from his golf account, although there was a brief frisson when he suggested that it was Mum's inbred relatives who had caused the hoo-ha with their cut-price toffee so maybe she should pay with her Evening Classes account. That argument was shortlived and Dad is driving them to surgery after *Goldfinger*. It is a shame. The peace is rather pleasant. It is almost *House on the Prairie*-like. Except with less bear-killing and more people saying things like, 'Ooh, isn't Sean Connery hairy.'

3 p.m.
The dogs are unstuck. And slightly dazed. At a cost of £200. James asked what miracle method Mr Mercer had used (he is hoping to patent it for forthcoming dog toffee incidents). Dad said a sharp pokey thing and a chisel. It is hardly the height of medical advancement.

. . . .

Thursday 27
Even I cannot take any more festive Clegg activity. Am

escaping to Scarlet's to exchange gifts. Sad Ed is collecting me in ten minutes. He is texting from behind the hedge to alert me to his arrival though. It is because last time he saw Granny Clegg she told him he looked like a young Geoff Capes and admired the 'meat' on him. He says she is detrimental to his self-esteem. Which is already dangerously low.

5 p.m.
Hurrah. Got an ironic Charlie and Lola diary from Scarlet. It is excellent thoughtful gift. Got Selection Box from Sad Ed. Which is nice, but potentially less thoughtful. Especially as he knows I do not like the Twirl or the Boost. Have given them to him already as extra gift. Although he is already pleased with his creatine. And has his eyes on Scarlet's Vitamin D as well. He says potentially he could overdose on either and achieve untimely death relatively painlessly. Watched essential Christmas film *Gremlins* (not *It's A Wonderful Life,* as I had thought) in the den with Jack, Bob, and Suzy. I said Suzy looked remarkably well, given that she must have been working tirelessly over the festive period. Suzy said it is down to a healthy diet of sex and Bellinis. And having Marks and Spencer make the nut roast, potatoes, gravy, and pudding. They are so forward-thinking. Anyway, have been invited to their annual New Year's Eve party. So has Hilary. Did not tell Scarlet about Justin thing. Think am not going to go. Cannot forsake best friend on crucial

night of year for cheap meaningless pact-breaking snog. Scarlet would never do anything like that to me.

10 p.m.
Would she?

. . . .

Friday 28

There is more Clegg-related chaos at home. This time Bruce's head is stuck behind a radiator. Which would not be so bad except the heating is on timer and due on any minute and only Mum knows how to work the controls and she is at Marjory's with strict instructions not to disturb her under any circumstances. Dad is trying to grease him out with some Swarfega. Have decided to pay emergency visit to exiled Rileys on Whiteshot Estate, i.e. Grandpa Riley, child bride Treena Riley, and Baby Jesus Harvey Nichols Riley. James is coming too. And the dog. They are all weary of the Cornish immigrants. They just do not understand our more civilized way of life. Plus the festive season is officially over at Summerdale Road. The tree is down and 'Now That's What I Call Christmas' is banned. Mum says she does not want to see another Quality Street or hear Noddy Holder shriek 'It's Christmas' for at least twelve months.

5 p.m.
Thank God for semi-chav relatives. It is still utterly festive

at 19 Harvey Road. In fact, cannot move in living room without getting partially strangled on foil paper chains. There was a minor issue when the dog panicked at Baby Jesus's outfit of choice (it is Power Ranger, he got it for his birthday off Donna). But Grandpa gave him a Baileys chocolate liqueur and he calmed down considerably. So have spent pleasant six hours eating Wagon Wheels and playing Treena's new 'Sounds of the 80s' DVD quiz. James won. There is nothing he does not know. (Except the ongoing why does Aladdin not have nipples question.)

Saturday 29

Oh my God. Have seen a ghost. Not a real one, or would be calling James into action with his revived ghostometer, but metaphorical one, on the vitamin aisle at Nuts In May. It is Tuesday Weeks, daughter of Dad's ex-girlfriend alcoholic Weirdy Edie, niece of ineffectual headmaster Mr Wilmott, and ex-lover of second best friend with suicidal tendencies and upper arm issues Sad Ed. I demanded to know what she was doing in this hick town. She said, 'Buying drugs, there's no law against it. Or is there now in this tinpot island?' She is so American, i.e. utterly unable to understand irony. Cannot believe I ever envied her. Anyway, I said not in here, I mean in the bigger sense, i.e. in Saffron Walden, home of previous love of your life. She said, oh that. Apparently she is back at Mr Wilmott's for a few days while Edie is on a spa break in

Arizona. She means rehab. Again. I said I hoped she wasn't thinking of coming to Scarlet's New Year's Eve party as the stress could send Sad Ed over the edge again. She said *au contraire*, Suzy had already invited her. And besides, it has been four months and is utterly pathetic that Sad Ed is still moping around over her. I said he is not, he has embraced a Simple Life and is devoting himself to more important matters. But she was already halfway up King Street by that point. Will not tell Sad Ed. Will just keep them in separate rooms. It is a big house. He need never know.

. . . .

Sunday 30

Thank God Hilary is coming tomorrow. It is not just that I am keen to see him, what with our excellent platonic relationship. It is that the Cleggs are driving everyone mad with their discovery of QVC on our Freeview box. It is like shopping at Trago Mills from the comfort of the sofa. So far they have bought a Lean Mean Grilling Machine (though do not think you can grill fishfingers or pie in this manner) and a set of three fitballs (for Bruce).

Scarlet has rung twice to check that Hilary is coming to the party. Which is very kind. Although a bit overkeen, as I pointed out. She said she is not overkeen, and anyway, why am I bothered? I said I am not bothered. She said nor is she and put the phone down. Which is odd, as have checked diary and she should not be premenstrual for at least three days. But am trying to banish unseasonal Doubting Riley thoughts as Christmas is time of goodwill to all men, and especially women.

· ·

Monday 31

New Year's Eve

Hurrah. It is New Year's Eve. And am feeling utterly jubilant as have checked resolutions (i.e. from birthday, not from last New Year as am totally different person now, i.e. not in the thrall of two-timing meat-mincing small-nippled philanderer, albeit with nice hair) and have fulfilled all of them, i.e. have not mooned about over Justin, have remained true to Scarlet above all others, and have utterly remembered that I, Rachel Riley, am responsible for my own happiness.

The Simple Life has been brilliant. In fact, will get Scarlet and Sad Ed to reswear our pact tonight. May even get Hilary to join in. He is due at five. (He rang from Chieveley services to advise on arrival times. He is trying to stay in my mum's good books after I warned him she is holding him partially responsible for the week's events due to his key role as chauffeur. It is because James said he was like Charon, i.e. ferrying the evil dead across the Styx to hell.) Hilary says we can go straight to Scarlet's if I like. This is an excellent plan. Especially as need to install ourselves in Scarlet's bedroom, possibly with locked door, to avoid Sad Ed and Tuesday encounter and potential untimely death.

10 p.m.

Hurrah. We are in Scarlet's bedroom in an utterly Simple Life style New Year celebration. Plus we have all renewed our vows not to do any snogging. Ever. Scarlet seemed a bit hesitant. But once Hilary had led the way she agreed. Jack said we are all mental and that there is no way any of us will stick to it. He is wrong. We are utterly united in our stance. And do not care that just yards away half of Saffron Walden is snogging under Suzy's sustainable mistletoe. We are missing nothing. And anyway, Hilary can tell us what is going on when he gets back from the toilet.

10.10 p.m.

Have just reinforced my anti-men stance to Scarlet. She said, 'Do you really not fancy Hilary at all?' I said, neither his brain nor his biceps were of interest to me in anything other than a platonic way. In fact, I do not fancy any men at all. Or women for that matter (have felt no urges despite trying to fantasize about Oona in a Kurt Cobain T-shirt several times). Jack said 'Are you sure, you really don't like anybody?' I said no. And Scarlet said, 'Good for you.' Which it utterly is.

10.20 p.m.

Jack has gone back to party and Scarlet has gone for an emergency wee. I pointed out that Hilary is not back yet so there will be no room. She said she will use the ensuite in Suzy's. She is mad. There is bound to be someone in there doing drugs or sex. Or both.

11.00 p.m.
Scarlet and Hilary are still not back. I fear they may have fallen foul of malign influences, i.e. Suzy. Sad Ed says we should go after them. Am in utter quandary as on one hand, do not think can cope on my own if Sad Ed bumps into Tuesday but on other, have to stop Scarlet failing in pact and trying to snog Hilary.

11.10 p.m.
Have decided to stay here. It is sisterlike thing to do. Even if Scarlet were to fall foul of her urges and try to break the pact, Hilary will be immune to her advances as it is obvious I am more his type. Plus Ed is not actually worried about Scarlet. He has run out of Pringles and wants to replenish his supply. Have texted Jack to bring some up.

11.30 p.m.
Thank God Jack is such loyal friend. The Pringles have proved essential. It is Sad Ed. He has had a turn for the worse. It is not the sensory deprivation at being shut in a black-painted goth shrine, it is evil Tuesday. She wandered into Scarlet's room on the pretext of looking for a bong. She is such a liar. She just wanted to flaunt her lipstick lesbian look in front of Sad Ed to torment him. So slammed door in her face in excellently dramatic manner.

(There are times when being sisterhoody is pointless.) But it was too late. Sad Ed had gone all white and breathless so had to sit him down and force BBQ Pringles into his mouth to revive him. He is a bit better now that his sugar and salt levels are up. But is decidedly minty about me not telling him she was back. I said he was utterly ungrateful and that he is lucky to have me, i.e. I am not keeping him here for my amusement. It is for his own good. He said, 'You're right. She is bad for me. Utterly bad.' He is resolved to stay with me until midnight. And then we will depart in a dignified manner. Out of Scarlet's window.

11.50 p.m.
Sad Ed has gone. And in a totally undignified manner, i.e. down the stairs shouting 'Tuesday!' at the top of his voice. It is flesh again. And his mind. They are both utterly weak.

11.55 p.m.
Jack has just been in to tell me to stop being an idiot and go downstairs for the midnight bongs (clock, not drugs, although with Suzy, anything is possible). Have refused. I will stay strong. I do not need the company of men. Not him, or Hilary, or Justin. I need only myself.

11.59 p.m.
Oh God. Cannot do this. Am going downstairs for reckless snogging. It is pointless to deny it any longer. I cannot live

without love. I have just been sticking my head in sand for the sake of a stupid pact. Hilary is my ONE. And if he refuses, there's always Justin. Or even Jack, as a last resort. Yes, have made mind up. The so-called Simple Life is not all it is cracked up to be after all. In fact, I quite like life being complicated. Scarlet will understand.

Anyway, it is a New Year. And new rules apply . . .

Joanna Nadin was born in Northampton and moved to Saffron Walden in Essex when she was three. She did well at school (being a terrible swot) and then went to Hull University to study Drama. Three years of pretending to be a toaster and pretending to like Fellini films put her off the theatre for life. She moved to London to study for an MA in Political Communications and after a few years as an autocue girl and a radio newsreader got a job with the Labour Party as a campaigns writer and Special Adviser. She now lives in Bath with her daughter and is a freelance government speech writer and TV scriptwriter. She has written five books for younger readers, several of which have been shortlisted for awards. *My (Not So) Simple Life* is her fourth book for Oxford University Press.

Liked

my (not s♥)

simple life?

Then visit

www.rachel-riley.com

for more about Rachel and her friends,
competitions and games.

Plus check out the author blog,
have your say, and join up to our
email bulletin for regular updates.

Have you read Rachel's first diary yet?

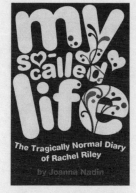

The Tragically Normal Diary of Rachel Riley

by Joanna Nadin

ISBN 978-0-19-275526-1

I need more tragedy in my life.

Why is life never like it is in books?
Nothing Jacqueline Wilson ever happens to me: I am not adopted,
my mum is not tattooed, I am not likely to move to the middle of a
council estate or be put into care. My parents are not alcoholics,
drug addicts or closet transvestites. Even my name is pants.

In other words, my life is earth-shatteringly NORMAL.

This cannot go on. Something deep and life-changing has to happen.
This year I shall befriend more exotic and interesting people, learn
to drink coffee (tragic heroines do not start the day with Cheerios
and lemon barley) and capture the heart of Justin Statham with my
vintage clothing and knowledge of all-time great guitar solos.

It's time for my so-called life to be brought up to speed. Starting now.

Rachel's diary continues in . . .

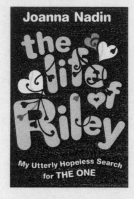

Joanna Nadin

the life of Riley

My Utterly Hopeless Search for THE ONE

ISBN 978-0-19-275527-8

My quest to find THE ONE starts right now!

This year I will utterly not snog random posh boys with congenital acne but will save myself for long-haired creative type with interest in tragicness and with musical potential i.e. Justin Statham. Though am not sure Justin has realized yet that I am THE ONE for him. Maybe he has heard I am rubbish at snogging.

I need to learn to SNOG properly – and fast.

Though perhaps I am just generally unlovable. As well as tongue technique issues I have hopelessly untragic relatives and a dog who eats furniture. Plus I am practically a medical midget and my hair is mental.

Maybe I should just give up on boys altogether . . .

Rachel's back in . . .

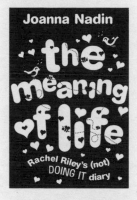

Joanna Nadin

the meaning of life

Rachel Riley's (not)
DOING IT diary

ISBN 978-0-19-272833-3

Am ready for year of utter LOVE!

It is official. I am going out with rock god and part-time meat mincer Justin Statham. Am certain that he is **THE ONE** and will prove it by having excellent relationship on every level.

Oh no. What if he wants me to do it?

Have only just got to grips with art of snogging so will need to get help fast. Or at least by 16th birthday. If **it** happens it needs to be earth-shattering and meaningful as **it** is, after all, the **Meaning of Life.**

Thank goodness I have definitely found **love of my life** and am not hung up on Jack any more. **Not** at all...